OUTRAGEOUS DECEPTION

After a hit-and-run accident, the unconscious victim is identified as Melissa Fielding, but as recovery begins, she feels detached from all around her: her handsome boy-friend; her job in his prestigious wine importing and exporting busi-ness; her past, risky lifestyle that is starting to catch up with her — even her name — none of it is familiar to her. As her memory returns, she risks losing all she has gained in order to discover the truth.

KAREN ABBOTT

OUTRAGEOUS DECEPTION

Complete and Unabridged

LINFORD
Leicester

First published in Great Britain in 2003

First Linford Edition
published 2004

British Library CIP Data

Abbott, Karen
Outrageous deception.—Large print ed.—
Linford romance library
1. Love stories
2. Large type books
I. Title
823.9'14 [F]

ISBN 1–84395–448–6

Published by
F. A. Thorpe (Publishing)
Anstey, Leicestershire

Set by Words & Graphics Ltd.
Anstey, Leicestershire
Printed and bound in Great Britain by
T. J. International Ltd., Padstow, Cornwall

This book is printed on acid-free paper

1

The Air France jet cruised along its flight path heading for Manchester Airport. Halfway along the aircraft, Melissa Fielding gazed out of the window, not really seeing the layer of white clouds below them.

She'd had three wonderful weeks in Southern France. Two of them had been spent at an international convention of wine merchants, where the boring business talk had been enjoyably broken by hours of relaxation, mostly on the beaches or by the pool during the day and a variety of nightclubs in the evenings. The third week, one she would have to justify in person on her return to England, had been total relaxation and pleasure.

Her pink lips pouted in rueful anticipation of the row likely to break out on her return. Trent would want a good explanation, and she would be seeing him tonight. She had better think of a reasonable story! Memories of the final week put a gleam into her blue eyes. Why shouldn't she have stayed on! The hotel had offered the third week at half price, as part of a holiday deal, but charging for meals taken on the premises, most of which hadn't landed on her bill!

She thought longingly of the last few days, spent mostly in Damien's arms, sunbathing on the beach, bathing in the pool, dancing the nights away at the discos, all heady stuff. It had been a wrench to tear herself away, and for what? To tell Trent it was over? Her expression tensed. The truth was, she didn't really know. Which should she choose? Security with Trent or passion with Damien?

Damien had been very persuasive. He had nearly convinced her to delay her return indefinitely. Her full lips curved upwards as she thought of him; tall, olive-skinned, slender body, dark,

dark eyes that seemed almost black, and the most sensual mouth she had ever kissed! The memory stirred a longing in her heart. Manchester or Marseille? Trent or Damien? Which should she choose?

She tucked some strands of her blonde hair behind her left ear. There was also that other matter to deal with back home. Her face became serious for a moment. She wasn't looking forward to facing that. In fact, given half a chance, she would do her best to avoid having to deal with it. She shouldn't have let it get to this stage. If only she knew what to do about Trent or Damien, then she needn't have to face it at all.

Thank goodness she had persuaded Trent not to meet her at the airport. That gave her time to consider what to do for the best and sort out her story. Another week! That was all she needed!

A British Airways airliner was also heading for Manchester Airport.

Madeleine Fielding tucked the novel

she had been reading into her handbag and looked out of the window in anticipation. She was looking forward to a couple of months break before she sought new employment.

She had had a wonderful year in Italy. It had been a chance of a lifetime, too good to miss, when she had had the opportunity to accompany Fabia Romayne to Rome, to be her companion/secretary whilst Fabia wrote the autobiography of her life in the world of fashion. But that was completed now, and Fabia had finally agreed to marry Cesare Galliano, a long-standing friend, to live out the remainder of her years in peaceful obscurity. It had been a wonderful wedding! Even the television crews had been there, filming for some documentary or other.

Madeleine thought fleetingly of Fabia's offer to keep her on in some vaguely-titled rôle but Madeleine had decided against it. It would have been very pleasant, but she knew she needed something more demanding, something to challenge her, though precisely what, she didn't yet know.

They were only a few minutes away from touchdown. Madeleine took out her make-up bag to add a spot of pink lipstick to her lips. It looked well against her tanned complexion and her blue eyes seemed even bluer. She absently tucked some strands of her blonde hair behind her right ear. It was a pity their parents were away on holiday, a whole month on a world cruise her mum had won in a competition. She replaced her make-up in her bag and fastened her seat belt. She wondered where Melissa, her identical twin, was. They had been very close at one time but had drifted apart since their teenage years. Now, at twenty-three, they hadn't seen each other for just over a year, shortly before she flew to Italy.

Madeleine decided to get in touch with her as soon as she had settled in at home. Their parents would be pleased to know they had been in touch, and so would she. Surely Melissa had become more steady, what with her responsible job and the opportunities it gave her. She hoped so. It had been Melissa's wild living that had driven a wedge between them in the first place, and it was time the rift was healed.

The airport was crowded. The holiday season was at its height.

Madeleine collected her flight bag and made her way towards the taxi rank. Maybe she should ring Melissa straight away. She worked here in Manchester at the moment, or had been doing so when they were last in touch. Nearly six months was a long time for Melissa to keep to one job. Madeleine took out her mobile phone and switched it on. She had barely tapped in the first two numbers when she heard her name shrieked.

'Maddie!'

She whirled round.

'Mel! Of all things! I was just telephoning you!'

The two young women flew into each

6

other's arms, hugging the life out of each other. Any signs of their recent estrangement were obliterated by their joy at seeing each other. Madeleine drew back first, standing back to take a good look at her twin.

'You look great, Mel. What are you doing here? Have you been away?'

'Yes. Southern France, for three weeks! It was fantastic. And you? Is this just a quick visit, or are you home for good?'

Madeleine quickly brought Mel up to date with her plans, adding wryly, 'I see we still do things the same, Mel. Even our flight bags are identical! I wonder if the items are the same as well?'

Melissa laughed.

'I doubt it, unless you've taken to wearing skimpy bikinis that barely cover your modesty!'

'You would probably call my bikinis too respectable!' Madeleine laughed in good nature. 'I've been with people who are mainly in a different age bracket from us.'

She looked at Melissa, trying to imagine her at some of the formal dinner parties she had attended in her capacity as Fabia's companion. No, Melissa wouldn't have fitted in! The place would have been in an uproar. They looked so alike, yet they were worlds apart in character. Perhaps they had changed even more.

'Do you think people will still have the same trouble knowing which of us is which?' she mused. 'Even Mum and Dad don't always get it right! Have you seen them recently, by the way?'

Mel had the grace to look slightly ashamed.

'Not for a few months. I was a bit tied up at work, and then my holiday cropped up. Still,' she added brightly, 'we can soon put that right! Or, better still, why don't you turn up and pretend to be me? I have got rather pressing business to deal with before I visit them.'

She took in Maddie's shocked expression.

'Oh, go on, Maddie! We used to do it a lot!'

Madeleine's smile had faded.

'We were children then, Mel. We played tricks, light-hearted tricks. This would be pure deception and I won't do it! Besides, they aren't there at the moment. They're on holiday. Didn't you know?'

'No, why should I? Anyway, you always were a spoilsport! I see you haven't changed! Why don't you loosen up a bit? You'd have more fun.'

'I doubt it, Mel. Anyway, it's too outrageous. Why don't we arrange for you to come for a visit when they come home from their holiday? It's ages since Mum and Dad saw both of us together. We could tease them a little then, swap clothes or something, to see if they can tell us apart!'

Melissa was already shaking her head.

'I'll have to think about that. I'm not sure what I'll be doing in the near future. There's someone I have to see here in Manchester, and then I've got to sweet-talk Trent into funding my extra week's holiday, so I need to get home to see him. I've time for a coffee, though. Let's share a taxi to the city centre and catch up on what we've been doing since we last met.'

'Great!'

Madeleine tucked her free hand into her twin's arm.

'And you can tell me all about this Trent you've mentioned.'

They slipped on to high stools in the restaurant they decided on and ordered a slice of chocolate gateau and cappuccino coffee each, grinning once again at their identical choice. Half an hour passed too quickly. Again, it was Melissa who looked at her watch.

'Well, dearest twin of mine, I must love you and leave you. How will you get home?'

'Train to Wigan, then taxi, I think. How about you?'

'Oh, it's a local visit,' Melissa said vaguely. 'I'll walk towards the station with you, until our routes diverge. It'll give us longer together, won't it?'

Five minutes later, they said their goodbyes, hugged and parted, promising to be in touch as soon as possible. Neither of them heard the car approaching the corner far too fast until it was too late to do anything about it. There was a horrendous squeal of brakes, a bang and a thud — and then, an unnatural silence.

2

The world was full of pain, unrelenting pain. The light hurt, and the darkness was terrifying. Her body hurt all over. Sometimes the pain faded but it always came screaming back, and, every so often, a terrifying bang sounded in her ears.

It made her whole body coil with tension as she waited for the blow that had catapulted her into this world of madness. But it didn't come. How could it, when it was there all the time?

'She's coming round,' a voice said. 'Hello, Melissa. Can you hear me?'

The voice came and went in an undulating rhythm, each word echoing over the next word spoken. She tried to open her eyes but they felt too heavy. She felt a hand squeeze hers.

'Can you feel this, Melissa? Try to squeeze my hand if you can.'

She tensed her muscles in her hand and tried to squeeze.

She must have managed it because the voice said, 'That's good, Melissa. Don't worry. I'll be back later.'

'Hello, Melissa,' a deeper voice said this time, though just as intrusive. 'We're just going to turn you a little. On my count . . . one, two, three.'

She felt herself lifted and put down again, sending waves of nausea flowing through her.

'Good afternoon, Melissa.'

Why couldn't they leave her alone? She wanted to drift away to a dark world somewhere just out of reach where the pain would leave her and she'd be able to get better . . .

Trent Gresham paced the floor of his flat. He had telephoned Manchester Airport and the plane had landed on time, so where was Melissa? Not for the first time, he regretted not meeting her at the airport, but she had been so insistent that he didn't. What was she up to? Had she decided to take yet another week's holiday, and only let him know at the last minute, like she had done last week? He grimaced slightly. At least her non-appearance would make his decision to end their relationship a bit easier when she finally did turn up. He had had enough.

He stood and looked out of the window. It overlooked the well-kept formal garden that surrounded the large complex. The night was still early. He was going out. If Melissa needed him, she had his mobile number and she could get in touch on that.

By mid-day on the Sunday, he didn't know whether to be angry or apprehensive. Surely if Melissa didn't intend to come back, she would at least send for her things.

On Monday morning, he fended off questions about her non-appearance at the wine merchant business that he owned, not wanting to spread rumours of their break-up before he had a chance to speak to Melissa first.

That evening, he decided that not

even Melissa would leave it this long to get in touch with him. He began to telephone the local hospitals, and was glad that he had done so. Melissa had been the victim of a hit-and-run accident. He felt himself to be a low-down rat for having thought badly of her, when she was lying unconscious and injured in hospital.

* * *

The pain was still there but seemed more bearable. She just wanted to be left alone to sleep.

'Hello, darling. Just you hang on in there. You're doing fine.'

Someone was calling her darling! She struggled to force open her eyes. For a moment, she succeeded. Hovering above her was a handsome, tanned, out-of-focus male face. His mouth was curved into a wide smile that seemed to surge forwards and backwards as she tried to focus upon it. Finding it impossible, she let her eyelids close again, hoping that the owner of the lovely smile would be there when she awoke again.

He wasn't, not the next time, nor the next, and she felt an awful sense of disappointment flood through her. If only he would come back, she knew she would gather together the strength to open her eyes.

'Hello, Melissa. How are you today? I've brought you some flowers. Would you like to see them?'

It was him, the owner of the smile! His voice reached down into her subconscious mind and drew her upwards, out of the cloying unreality that weighed heavily upon her. Her eyelids flickered and opened.

He was sitting on the edge of her bed, smiling down at her. She didn't know him but he seemed to know her. She wished she did know him. His smile warmed her body, melting the grip of ice within her.

His hair was dark brown, almost black. It was cut quite short and was brushed backwards, though a small lock at the front curled wilfully over his forehead. His eyes were the colour of burned almonds and, in spite of his smile, they held a hint of anxiety. He had a firm mouth but now, as her gaze remained constant, his lips parted slightly, revealing perfect white teeth.

The sight of his smile tugged somewhere deep inside her. He was looking at her as if she meant something to him and she was afraid his smile would fade when he knew that she didn't know him.

'Welcome back, Melissa.'

His voice was warm and vibrant. It made her want to respond.

'Is that my name?' she croaked through cracked lips.

Her voice sounded strange to her ears. Why couldn't she speak properly?

'Yes, Miss Melissa Fielding, spinster of this parish!' he joked.

She let the name settle in her mind. Melissa Fielding. She didn't feel like a Melissa Fielding, but whom did she feel like? Nothing came to mind.

'What's your name?' she asked hesitantly, not wanting to destroy the rapport between them, but knowing that she had to be honest with him.

'Trent Gresham, bachelor extraordinaire!'

'Do I know you?'

'You sure do, honey! I'm your boss and . . . well . . . very close friend.'

She weighed his words. He seemed very sure of himself. She felt she could trust him. She wondered just how close they were but didn't feel it was quite the time to ask. There was so much uncertainty within her. Where was she? Why couldn't she move? Why didn't she know this man, or even know herself?

She suddenly realised that she knew nothing about herself, not only her name, but everything! Who was she? What did she do? Where did she live? What sort of things did she like?

'I don't know anything!' she whispered.

Panic was rising within her. She

reached out towards him and was grateful when he clasped hold of her hand. She held on to him tightly.

'It's all right,' he soothed her. 'You were in a bit of an accident and banged your head. Apart from some bruising, you're not too badly hurt. Another couple of days in hospital and you should be ready to come home.'

'With you?'

He smiled.

'Well, yes. Don't you want to?'

He said it teasingly, but she sensed an uncertainty about the question.

'Is that where I live?'

'You have done so for the past four months.'

'Oh.'

Why couldn't she remember?

'Don't worry. The doctor said this might happen. Your memory will come back soon. You're suffering from concussion. The doctor says that being back in your own environment should help you to remember.'

'What happened to me? You said an

accident. Was I in a car?'

'No. You were walking along the pavement. It seems a car mounted the pavement and ran you down. The driver didn't stop. You were brought here in an ambulance.'

'How did everyone know who I am, and know to contact you?'

'You had just returned from France and your passport and other documents were in your bag, but not the address or phone number of the flat. I was worried when you didn't arrive home and I eventually began to ring round the various hospitals around Manchester. It was quite a shock when I struck lucky, I can tell you!'

'How long have I been here?'

'Four days.'

Four days! And she couldn't remember them!

'I'm frightened!'

Trent gathered her in his arms, regardless of the tubes that led to and from her.

'It's all right! I'll take care of you.

You'll soon remember! You just see if you don't!'

A nurse came bustling in.

'Now, now! You've set the beepers going!' she reproved them lightly. 'I think it's time Melissa rested again, Mr Gresham. We don't want her overdoing it, do we?'

She smiled brightly, making Melissa feel like a naughty child.

When Trent had left, she sank into her pillows. She had a lot to think about, she thought sleepily.

Three days later, on Saturday, Trent took her home to their flat, situated on the outskirts of Manchester. It was part of a purpose-built, luxury development. The courtyard was bright with tubs of flowers and hanging baskets. Melissa looked around admiringly. It had an air of opulence. A youth ran lightly down the steps from the foyer and Trent tossed him the keys to his car.

'Good afternoon, Mr Gresham. Good to see you home, Miss Fielding!'

Melissa smiled at him.

'Thank you.'

'Thanks, Alec,' Trent echoed. 'Alec takes care of the cars here,' he explained to Melissa, seeing her puzzled expression. 'He's a reliable worker, if you need anything when I'm not here.'

'Are you going away?'

'No, but I'll have to go out to work. I've taken today off but I'll have to go in tomorrow.'

Melissa felt sure she'd feel lost without him at her side but she didn't say so. She felt enough of a burden to him, this man with whom she had apparently lived for four months.

They had entered the luxuriously-furnished building. It resembled a five-star hotel more than a block of flats. A thick red carpet covered the floor. In the foyer, there were a number of deep armchairs set out, with small tables upon which rested bowls of flowers. Copies of famous paintings adorned the softly-papered walls. At least, Melissa deemed them to be copies.

She was very conscious of his presence beside her as they went up in the lift to the first floor. Even though Melissa didn't know anything about him apart from what he had told her in the past few days, she felt very drawn to him. His quiet air of authority gave her confidence.

The upstairs floor was just as grand as downstairs. A wide corridor spread out in two directions. Trent led her to the right. Spindle-legged tables nestled against the walls at regular intervals, supporting either yet more flowers or attractive ornaments. More paintings graced the walls, pastoral scenes up here. Melissa liked them. Trent paused outside an apartment and fitted his key into the lock.

'Your keys were missing from your purse,' he remarked. 'I'll have to get the locks changed, in case they were stolen whilst you were unconscious. You don't happen to know if you've left them somewhere, do you?'

Melissa shook her head. She didn't

remember anything of all this, never mind what had happened to her keys. She felt very nervous as Trent swung open the door and stepped aside to allow her to step in front of him. Surely her home would be familiar to her? It wasn't!

They had stepped into a wide hallway. Its main colour was white, though the carpet was a pale silver grey. Double doors with small glass panes led into a large-sized lounge. She looked around in dismay. Again the colour was white, the walls, the leather suite, the cushions. The carpet was the same silver grey colour. The few items of furniture were of chrome and glass. The only splash of colour in the room was the painting on one of the walls. It was a white background with a splash of bright red, just off-centre.

She mustn't have had anything to do with the choosing of the décor. She wasn't sure what her taste might be, but it wasn't this! How could she have lived here for four months and not recognise any of it? She realised that Trent was watching her reaction and knew she had disappointed him. She looked at him helplessly.

'It's very nice,' she said weakly, 'but I don't remember it.'

'Never mind! It's early days yet! What do you want to do first? Have a cup of tea or something? Or have the guided tour?'

She managed a smile.

'The guided tour, please. I don't think I like tea.'

He looked surprised.

'Don't you? You've drunk enough of it in the past! Probably it's the hospital variety that has put you off! Come on. I'll show you round, then you'd better have a rest. And stop looking so guilty! You can't help losing your memory.'

He sounded a bit impatient and Melissa pulled herself together. He was right. She couldn't help it, and it would come back!

The kitchen was pristinely hygienic . . . more chrome . . . more white units, and sparsely-filled cupboards.

'I take it I don't cook much!' she joked.

'You could say that! But then, neither do I!'

'How do we survive?'

'There's a good meals service in the area, and plenty of eating places. You'll soon get back into the swing of it.'

The dining-room had ebony furniture, contrasting with the white walls. A stereo system graced one corner and glass-fronted cupboards were seen to hold a pure white dinner service and expensive-looking ornaments.

The bathroom was plush with a deep-piled white carpet, large, sunken, corner bath with Jacuzzi, a walk-in shower, bidet and toilet. The colours were white and gold. Thick white towels hung from the heated rail. A large, trailing green plant sat on the side of the bath, adding some relief from the interminable white. Two smaller rooms were a guest room and an office.

'And the master bedroom!' Trent said with a flourish.

It was stark and masculine, though the bed looked very comfortable and inviting. Melissa stood stiffly in the doorway and swallowed hard. What would Trent expect of her? She didn't know him! She couldn't restrain a small sound of distress and she turned blindly away from the bed.

Trent was standing close behind her and he gathered her into his arms as she turned into him. He nestled his face into her hair.

'It's all right,' he murmured. 'I'll sleep in the guest-room for now, as long as you don't mind me coming in here for clothes. I promise to knock!'

Melissa managed a smile.

'I'd appreciate that, as long as you don't mind. It's just . . . '

She paused. She didn't know what to say. Trent was being so understanding, but he still seemed like a total stranger to her. In spite of that, she already felt a warmth towards him, a sense of belonging, when she was in his arms. Her feelings would return, she was sure, but how long would Trent be prepared to wait?

'Come on. I'll make you a cup of coffee. Your usual cappuccino?'

'If you say so,' she replied. 'It feels funny not knowing what I like or don't like! I'll have to learn all over again.'

'The doctor said your memory will come back gradually and not to become anxious about it. We'll work at it together.'

'You're very kind to me. I don't know what I'd be doing without you.'

She followed him into the kitchen and watched as he made the coffee.

'Haven't I any family? I mean, no-one seems to have missed me, or, if they have, they haven't managed to trace me. Do you think I might be on a missing persons' list somewhere?'

Trent carried the two cups of cappuccino into the lounge and placed them on the glass and chrome coffee table.

'You haven't got any family, I'm afraid.'

He hesitated and looked down at his hands.

'I'm sorry if this is a shock to you, but your parents died in a plane crash two years ago, and you've no brothers and sisters. You haven't mentioned aunts and uncles or grandparents but, if you have any, you aren't in immediate touch with them.'

He leaned forwards and gently took hold of her hands.

'I'm sorry to break it to you like this. I don't know if it's been the right thing to do, but you'll probably start to remember it all soon.'

Melissa felt very lonely for a moment. Without any family and no memories of them, what was there to build her life on? Her natural commonsense came to her aid and she squeezed his hands gratefully.

'There's no point me grieving about them. I presume I have already done that.'

She reached for the mug of cappuccino and tentatively sipped it. She raised the mug in salute.

'You're right, this time. This is lovely.'

'Good! I'm glad you like it.'

His eyes crinkled at the corners and Melissa felt a glow of warmth wrap itself around her. His chin had a slight cleft, which deepened when he smiled. She couldn't help feeling how fortunate she was to have him looking after her so faithfully.

'Now, about this evening. I thought I'd send out for a meal. Is that all right? I expect you're feeling a bit overwhelmed with everything that's new to you here. We can watch a video later, if you wish, and then you'll probably want an early night.'

He looked questioningly at her, and she nodded gratefully.

'Thank you, that sounds lovely.'

She felt so inadequate.

'What would we normally have been doing?'

'Oh, a meal out, sometimes with

friends . . . the theatre . . . a nightclub. Sometimes we go away for the week-end.'

'I feel I'm spoiling your weekend.'

'Nonsense! It's a refreshing change to spend it quietly. You're normally rushing me off to nightclubs and making me feel twice my age! Not that I mind!' he hastened to assure her. 'It's a pleasure to be your escort! I see other fellows looking at you, wishing you were with them, but you're with me! You're generally the star of the show.'

She felt genuine surprise. She didn't feel like a star. It suddenly occurred to her that she hadn't the slightest idea what she looked like. She hadn't thought to ask for a mirror at the hospital.

'I think I need to freshen up,' she said brightly, placing the empty mug on the table.

Trent stood up with her.

'Next to the bedroom,' he said. 'You'll find it.'

He took the empty mugs into the

kitchen while Melissa nervously made her way to the bathroom. She crossed over to the washbasin, almost afraid to raise her head to look at her reflection.

Come on, now, she told herself. You've just heard what Trent said. You make men turn their heads to watch you! She took a deep breath and raised her head. Her eyes stared wildly at the reflection of her bruised and swollen face, her hands flying to cover her cheeks. Who could love her with a face like that?

3

How could he? How could Trent have told her she was so beautiful that other men envied him? How cruel! She made herself lower her hands from in front of her face and look stony-faced at the mirror.

'I'm not beautiful,' she whispered. 'I'm ugly!'

No wonder Trent had suggested they buy a meal from the catering service! He was ashamed to be seen out with her! As the reflected image stared back at her, the bathroom door was pushed open and Trent, ashenfaced, stood in the doorway. He strode forward and took hold of her.

'Melissa! Forgive me. I didn't think! I'm so sorry! I knew you hadn't seen yourself, but I forgot. You poor darling, I'm so very, very sorry!'

Melissa pushed at his chest with her hands.

'How could you tell me that I'm beautiful?' she cried. 'Do you feel sorry for me? Well, I don't want your pity, or anyone else's!'

She struggled free from his arms and fled to the bedroom, where she flung herself face-down on to the bed and sobbed her heart out.

Trent stood staring out of the lounge window, not seeing the well-kept garden that surrounded Crompton Court. He closed his eyes and, for a moment, laid his forehead against the cool glass. How could he have been so thoughtless? It was no excuse that he had become accustomed over the past few days to the way she looked. He knew she still hadn't seen the bruising. The staff nurse had warned him and told him to prepare her gently. He thumped a fist into the palm of his other hand. Fool!

He knew her face was already better than it had been, but that was no consolation to Melissa. He had been shocked at the first sight of her, had barely recognised her, except for her lovely hair.

As his anger against himself cooled down, he reflected on how well Melissa had coped thus far. He had expected her to be far more histrionic. The shock of the accident had obviously taken its toll on her, subdued her. He smiled faintly. Life would be far more pleasant if she remained less volatile than her usual self. He was aware of a more tender attitude towards her, more like in the beginning when they were getting to know each other.

Well, he thought wryly, as he turned away from the window, it was delaying his decision to tell her that he wished to end their relationship. He couldn't do so whilst she was in so fragile a condition, and maybe he would grow to love her all over again.

Melissa had lost track of time as she lay on the bed. She sat up and pushed her hair off her face. She was going to have to get used to how she looked. She had been wrong to be so angry towards Trent. His distress had been genuine. She noticed that there was an en-suite bathroom leading off the bedroom. Bracing herself to accept what she saw, she crossed the room and looked at her reflection.

She tried to see past the disfigurement, to see if she could discern her true features, but found it impossible. Back in the bedroom, she pulled out her make-up purse and sat down on the low stool in front of the dressing-table. Beginning with a small pot of cream, she gently smeared some over the worst of her bruises and then tentatively dabbed a little powder over her cheeks, disguising the vividness of the bruises. She added some light blue eye shadow, twirled the mascara stick on her eyelashes, and then carefully applied a light coating of dusky pink lipstick.

She leaned away from the mirror, critically examining her new reflection. It wasn't perfect but she looked better!

She was no longer some fearsome monster, about to scare the entire neighbourhood! A hopeful smile hovered over her lips. Trent was right. It would get better. At least there were no scars to worry about. She had been very lucky.

Whilst the buoyant air was upon her, she nervously returned to the lounge. Trent was still there, seated on the sofa, reading the newspaper. She paused in the doorway.

'How do I look?'

Trent immediately put down his paper and rose to his feet. He held out his arms towards her and she moved forward.

'You look wonderful!' he complimented her.

She laughed shakily.

'I wouldn't win a beauty contest!'

'You will in time.'

'I can't remember what I should look like. Have you a photograph of me? I feel I am looking at a stranger when I look in the mirror.'

'Are you sure? I mean, it won't upset you, will it?'

'It can't upset me any more than seeing myself looking like this!'

'All right, then. We had our photograph taken at the firm's summer dinner party. It's in my office.'

He left her standing in the lounge and soon returned holding a framed photograph. Melissa took it from him. She looked at the smiling couple. Trent was dressed in a black dinner suit, looking very handsome. Next to him, stood a very pretty young woman. Trent's arm was laid casually around her shoulders. She was dressed in a dark blue, low-cut evening gown that slid closely over her hips. Her hair was taken up on to the top of her head, where it was fastened in a loose waterfall of waves.

'Is that really me?' she asked in amazement.

'It is! What do you think of it?'

'My hair looks curly.'

'You spent hours in front of the

mirror with your curling wand,' he said with a reminiscent smile. 'I threatened to go without you!'

She studied the photograph, carefully examining her face. Her eyebrows puckered as a faint memory hovered just out of reach.

'Melissa,' she murmured, speaking her name softly.

She looked up at Trent. He was now standing behind her, looking at the photograph over her shoulder.

'It feels strange,' she admitted slowly. 'It's like looking at a picture of someone else. Yet I feel it's stirring my memory.'

She handed the photograph back to Trent with a rueful laugh.

'I can't remember the occasion. Did we have a good time?'

Trent thought of the row that had ended the evening. Melissa had had too much to drink but wouldn't accept his word for it. She made a public spectacle of them both right in the middle of the dance floor, until he had managed to lead her out to the taxi he had ordered.

He pushed the unpleasant memory aside. There was no point in reminding her. Some memories were better forgotten!

'Yes,' he said lightly. 'A memorable evening.'

She looked at him sharply but his expression was bland. Feeling happier with the way she now looked, she suddenly felt restless, and a little peckish.

'Do we have to eat in?' she asked. 'Isn't there anywhere where we can go dressed just as we are? Somewhere casual?'

With a smile of pleasure, Trent agreed.

'Why don't we go for a drive and call in at a pub somewhere? The weather promises to hold. It should be a pleasant evening.'

He drove around the north side of Bolton, taking the high road out to the moors. They parked at Belmont, and ate in the pub on the corner of the crossroads.

'Choose for me!' Melissa laughed, on reading the menu. 'You know my preferences more than I do! Let's see how good you are!'

They had Thai chicken dips for starters, a medium-grilled steak with chips and salad for main course, and a delicious chocolate dessert, all of which Melissa pronounced excellent.

'The best meal I remember!' she joked, as they returned to the car.

She was feeling happy with the way the evening had developed and was suddenly optimistic about her future. Her memory would return and she would soon be able to pick up the threads of her life.

It was quite late when they returned to Crompton Court and Melissa opted to go straight to bed. A short, satin nightdress was folded on one of the pillows and she retreated into the en-suite bathroom to shower and change. She felt guilty when Trent removed some of his clothes from one side of the fitted wardrobes and the chest of drawers but she was grateful.

The following day, she spent part of the morning unpacking her holiday flight bag that Trent had left for her to see to herself. She held up the skimpy summer dresses in front of her, trying to visualise them on her. They would certainly show her slim figure to advantage. There were slim-fitting, lightweight trousers and various cropped-tops to wear with them. The very brief bikinis almost made her blush, as did most of her underwear.

The next two days at home on her own nearly drove her to distraction. There was a definite limit as to how many magazines one could read to alleviate boredom.

'I need to be doing something,' she explained to Trent. 'Can't I come in to work with you? Maybe seeing where I spend most of my days will strike some memory chords.'

Trent agreed.

'Everyone knows about your accident,' he explained. 'They'll be sympathetic towards you.'

'What precisely do we do?' Melissa asked later, as she stood in front of a large red brick building in the heart of Manchester.

It had an imposing entrance. Two large, stone columns stood at the head of a short flight of stone steps. The heavy main front door was painted white. The three levels of outer windows were adorned with brightly coloured window boxes of various flowering plants.

'We are wine merchants. We import wines from other countries and sell them on to large supermarket chains and specialist shops.'

Melissa shook her head in wonderment. It sounded interesting but she couldn't recall any of it. Inside was relatively dark, most of the lower wall surfaces being covered with highly-polished dark wood. The higher portions of wall were painted cream. A glittering chandelier hung over the centre of the spacious hall and a magnificent staircase rose to the higher floors. Trent led the way up the first flight of stairs and turned into the first office.

'Good morning, ladies!'

'Good morning, Trent,' a chorus of replies responded to his cheerful greeting, followed by a less enthusiastic, 'Good morning, Melissa.'

One of the young women stepped forward.

'It's good to see you back again, Melissa. We were sorry to hear of your accident but relieved that it wasn't any worse.'

Her eyes flickered over Melissa's face but avoided making eye contact with her. Melissa felt her embarrassment.

'I do look rather a mess, don't I?' she said lightly, making herself smile cheerfully. 'You should see me without make-up on! One consolation is that it can only get better.'

The young woman looked gratified at

her humorous response.

'Would you like a cup of tea?' she offered. 'I'll get one of the girls to make you one.'

'That would be nice, Rebecca,' Trent answered for her. 'Make it two coffees though, would you?'

He turned to Melissa.

'Rebecca is in charge of the office,' he said quietly as Rebecca turned to pass on the request to one of the other girls. 'The others are Lauren, Emma and Nicola. You'll soon get to know them. That's your desk, over there by the window. Why don't you settle yourself down there and familiarise yourself with is contents? I just need to have a quick word with Rebecca.'

He moved away to where Rebecca had her desk and engaged himself in conversation with her, checking through the contents of a large ledger. With a hesitant smile at the other girls, Melissa seated herself at her desk. It looked very tidy, almost as if it hadn't been used for a while. Oh, of course! She'd been on holiday, hadn't she? Then there had been another week and a half recuperating. A computer sat in prime position. Presumably, she knew how to use it. She looked at the various buttons and pressed one at the side of the screen. A light glimmered but nothing else.

'Lauren, where do I switch it on?' she asked the girl at the next desk.

Lauren pressed her lips together. She looked as if she was going to say something but, with a sidelong glance to where Trent and Rebecca were still talking, she changed her mind.

'That button on the right,' she said shortly.

Melissa murmured her thanks, a little taken aback by the girl's attitude. She pressed the button indicated and sat back to watch the computer screen spring into life. Although she couldn't remember what the next sequence of changes on the screen meant, each change of screen seemed to be vaguely familiar as it happened. Eventually a message on the screen asked for her password. She hadn't a clue what it was!

The other three girls were busy typing away. Lauren was refusing to make any eye contact. The next girl, Emma, glanced across. Melissa smiled ruefully at her.

'I know this sounds ridiculous, but I don't know my password,' she confessed hesitantly.

A sound suspiciously like a snort sounded from Lauren's direction. Melissa glanced at her sharply, but the girl was intently rifling through a sheaf of papers and didn't respond. Melissa looked back at Emma.

'Does anyone else know it, Emma?'

Emma looked slightly embarrassed. She exchanged a swift glance with Nicola and Lauren.

'We aren't supposed to,' she admitted reluctantly, 'but you did rather make a big thing of it. Try, Cool Chick.'

'Thanks.'

Melissa laid her fingers on the keyboard. It felt comfortingly familiar.

She carefully typed the letters. The screen leaped into life and a bright yellow chicken began to strut across the screen, the words Cool Chick dancing behind it. Her smile faded as she read the words that followed — 'You get on our wick!'

She looked up sharply. The three girls had been watching her reaction but now looked away hastily.

'Someone's been busy!' Melissa said lightly.

'Just a joke,' Emma muttered, looking down at her work again.

Melissa forced herself to smile.

'Joke taken!'

She wondered if they regularly played jokes on each other, or was it just towards her? Didn't they like her for some reason?

Her fingers were running lightly over the keyboard. It felt familiar. She decided to play around for a few minutes. She laid her fingers on the keys, then closed her eyes and took some deep breaths to calm herself down. What should she type?

All she could remember were the events of the past few days, so she began to type out a sort of diary. At first, she kept looking for the correct keys but she soon realised that her fingers were on them before she had consciously found them. Feeling more confident, she typed more swiftly and soon had completed a page of her memories of her post-accident life.

Taking a chance that the tiny picture of what seemed to represent a sheet of paper in a typewriter was indeed what it portrayed itself to be, she clicked on to it and was gratified to hear the printer at her side buzz into life.

'Well, at least I can type!' she said aloud.

'Big deal!' Lauren muttered.

Melissa breathed deeply. She had to sort this out.

'Do you have a problem with me, Lauren?'

Lauren glanced at Nicola and Emma. She seemed as though she was going to evade answering but changed her mind.

'We all have a problem with you, if you must know!'

She looked around for support from the other two. Of the two, Nicola seemed to be in less agreement. Melissa addressed her.

'Is that so, Nicola?'

'You have been . . . well, sort of difficult to get along with.'

'And some!' Lauren snorted, tossing back her head.

Melissa felt her confidence ebb away.

'What have I done?' she asked quietly.

The three girls exchanged glances again. Emma shrugged.

'It's the way you speak to us and . . . well, you do rather take advantage of your position with the boss!'

Melissa listened quietly, feeling completely at a loss. She couldn't defend herself. Nothing she was hearing struck any memory chords.

4

Trent's return to the office prohibited any further devastating revelations about her character and Melissa was relieved when he suggested taking her on a tour of the building, although she knew it would reinforce the prejudice the girls already held against her.

'I'll see you all later, then,' she said with a false brightness in her voice.

She snatched up her bag and almost ran from the room.

'Are you all right?' Trent asked her in concern.

'Yes, of course! Why shouldn't I be?' she mumbled.

She mustn't cry! She had better get used to unexpected reactions from people, if what Nicola and Lauren had said about her was true! She wished she could slip into the ladies' room but didn't know where it was.

'It all just seems so strange,' she excused herself. 'People know things about me that I don't know myself!'

She looked up at him, wondering if he would reassure her that she had no need to worry, but he didn't.

'We all tread on a few toes at times,' he said ruefully. 'Your present problem is that you don't know whose toes you have stood on!'

Melissa halted abruptly and stared at him.

'Do I go around treading on people's toes as a regular habit?'

'You have a lively personality, Melissa. You're bound to rub some people up the wrong way.'

He smiled as he spoke, as if trying to lessen the statement.

'Is that a yes or a no?'

'Come on! I didn't start this.'

'Yes or no?'

He smiled lopsidedly at her and spread his hands.

'Maybe! Possibly! OK, yes! You have talent for it!'

She felt downcast as she considered his words.

'Do I tread on your toes?' she asked hesitantly.

Trent grimaced humorously.

'Sometimes!'

'But we're still together?'

'I'm a masochist!'

'Meaning?'

'Nothing! It was a joke!'

He drew her close and held her gently to him. His body was firm and protective and Melissa leaned into him. The spicy fragrance of his aftershave emphasised his masculinity. Melissa drew comfort from his gesture but she felt deeply troubled. She sensed that things weren't totally well between them and wondered if he was only there for her because of pity for her in her present condition. She bit back the challenge that sprang to her mind. It wasn't the place, and she needed time to think.

'It's been a bit of a culture shock for you,' Trent murmured as he stepped away and held her at arms' length.

He studied her face. He felt concerned about her. It couldn't have been easy for her, and, from the nature of her questions, the girls in the office had given her a hard time.

'Have you had enough? I can take you home if you wish.'

'No. I'm not going to run away. It would be all the harder to return tomorrow, which I fully intend to do. I'm not giving up at the first hurdle.'

She looked at her watch.

'It's turned twelve. Do we close for lunch, or could we go early? It would seem more like a natural break.'

He admired her courage. Had the accident somehow made her more sensitive to other people? He let his arm curl around her shoulders as he turned her in the direction of the main entrance.

'An excellent suggestion! I'm quite hungry myself and I know a nice little Italian place not too far away.'

It was nice! Melissa felt at home immediately. Trent led her to a corner table and held out the chair for her. She slid into place, grateful for the respite from the office. She wasn't especially hungry and chose a small portion of diced chicken in a tomato and rosemary sauce, served with a side salad. Trent chose a larger portion of the same, served with rice and salad. He ordered two glasses of wine.

She was grateful for his light conversation throughout the meal and tried to concentrate on what he was saying, rather than trying to plan what she might say to the girls when she returned to the office. She wasn't looking forward to it but she knew that, if she wished to continue to work there, she had to face the problem and try to rebuild her relationship with Emma, Nicola and Lauren.

She was the first to return to the office and was glad to have the opportunity to look around. She didn't touch any of the other girls' desks but concentrated on the notice boards and filing system.

Lauren was the next to return. She bristled immediately.

'Keep your nose out of my work!' she warned.

'Lauren!'

Emma had followed her in. She fixed Lauren with a significant look, nodding over towards Melissa's desk.

'Give her a break, like we said.'

'Yes, well!' Lauren screwed her face into a show of reluctant apology. 'Sorry, I suppose!'

'Why the change?' Melissa challenged. 'I don't want your pity.'

'It's not pity.'

Emma nodded towards the piece of paper on Melissa's desk.

'We ... er ... read your print-out. You're having a tough time. It can't be easy for you and we decided to wipe the slate clean, if you agree, that is.'

Nicola had joined them now and Melissa looked from one to the other. They seemed genuine and Nicola and

Emma at least were smiling.

'I honestly can't remember what has happened between us,' Melissa confessed, 'but, if I've upset you, then I'm sorry. I appreciate the new start.'

She held out her hand and each one took it in turn.

'If I start getting too big for my boots, I'll look to you to remind me to back off, Lauren,' she added with a rueful grin.

'Hmm, we'll see. Leopards and their spots and all that!'

'Anyway, Rebecca's told me to remind you about what you do,' Nicola informed Melissa.

Nicola joined her at her desk and good-naturedly went through part of their accounting system with her. Melissa listened carefully, trying in vain to find tags to grasp hold of. Eventually, though, she had to admit defeat.

'I can't make head nor tail of this!' she exclaimed. 'Are you sure I worked on the accounts? It was my sister who studied maths, not me!'

'You haven't got a sister!' Emma accused. 'At least, that's what you told us! Left all alone in the world when your parents died in an accident!'

Melissa frowned as she tried to hold on to the strand of a memory that had prompted her remark.

'Maybe my sister died in the same accident,' she said sadly, feeling the loss acutely.

She stared blankly into space, finding it hard to cope with. It was worse not knowing! She must have done the grieving once already, but now she was having to face it all again, bit by bit, and it wasn't easy.

'You know, I don't really think I'm going to be much use in here until my memory returns,' Melissa conceded eventually. 'I'm not only unable to help with the work, I'm actually a hindrance to you.'

She felt thoroughly deflated. So much for getting back to work as therapy! Yet, surely there was something she could do.

'The old Melissa would never have admitted that!' Emma remarked. 'I know it's hard luck on you, but I reckon that bang on your head has done you a good turn!'

'How can you say that? It's made me unemployable!' Melissa groaned. 'I may as well throw in the towel right now! Are there no openings for written work? It's like that print-out you read. I almost did that without thinking!'

'Not in here,' Lauren remarked, 'but I did hear Mr Gresham ask Rebecca if she had got anywhere with employing someone to create the new brochure.'

Melissa was all ears.

'What would that entail?'

'Don't ask me! I'm a mathematician!' Lauren replied.

'Which I'm not! At least, not at the moment! Can a bang on the head really change someone like that?'

'It's changed you!'

'So it seems. I think I need to talk to Trent.'

She grinned wickedly at the other girls.

'If I make you girls a cup of tea, will you promise not to call me for taking advantage of my position as Trent's girlfriend?'

'Just this once!'

Trent had been expecting a much-subdued Melissa to accompany him home. He had planned to take her out to dine and then to see a show, anything to distract her from her usual histrionics when things didn't go entirely to plan.

'That's sweet of you, Trent, but we need to talk,' she said.

'Talk, as in reasonable discussion?'

'What else?'

'Right! We'll dine, and talk.'

He found himself whistling as he showered in the main bathroom and dressed in a well-cut suit, not quite sure why he felt so light-hearted. Melissa was bearing up reasonably well, though he knew she was also finding life difficult. The accident must have really shaken her and made her aware of her own mortality. She was showing greater consideration to other people and, now, was willing to talk through her problems instead of demanding instant reparation. How long would it last?

His heart lurched when Melissa joined him in the lounge only five minutes after he was ready. She was dressed in a pale blue closely-fitting dress with shoestring straps. Her hair was hanging loosely but she had softened the style in some way that women seemed to know about and her make-up was minimal. She quite took his breath away.

'Sorry I took so long,' she apologised. 'I couldn't decide which dress to wear. I've so many!'

'You look wonderful. Come here.'

He rose to greet her and drew her into his arms. She stiffened slightly and, instead of kissing her as he had intended, he held her slightly away from him.

'I like your perfume,' he complimented.

Her shy look of pleasure entranced
him. He tilted her chin up towards him
and kissed her lips lightly. After an
initial freeze, he felt her relax into him,
her lips responding under his. As her
response deepened, he felt a sudden
guilt. He had promised to give her time
to readjust and here he was, pushing
their relationship forward. He straightened slowly.

'I think we'd better go out, or we may
not get there!' he said lightly.

The city centre was quiet, it being
mid-week. He had booked a table and
asked for a secluded place, not too sure
what Melissa's talking would entail. He
waited until they had placed their order
before he prompted her to begin. For a
few seconds she glanced down. When
she looked up, her face was serious, her
eyes slightly apprehensive.

'I didn't have too good a day today,'
she began. 'As you know, this morning
the girls gave me a rough time, but they

couldn't have been nicer in the afternoon, especially Emma and Nicola. Nicola spent some time showing me the ropes, but I honestly couldn't grasp hold of much of what she was trying to show me. I'm worse than a school-leaver at her first job!'

'It'll all come back. You must give it time.'

He reached across the table and took hold of her hand.

'You don't have to return to work yet. I could see what a strain it was for you. Why don't you spend some more time relaxing first?'

'No. I want to be there. I'm sure it will help me in the long run, but I'd prefer to be doing something different. I seem to be able to write my thoughts quite lucidly, and I wondered if there was something I could do in that line.'

'Such as?' Trent queried, raising an eyebrow.

'Well, Lauren said you are looking for someone to design a new brochure about the wines you sell. Do you think I could have a go at doing that?'

Trent couldn't hide his surprise.

'What do you know about wines?'

'Right now, not a lot! But I could learn and I presume that you have the information to go in the brochure.'

He realised he was still holding her hand.

'It needs someone who can design a layout, someone with a flair for words. I don't really think . . . '

'I'm not sure, but the thought excites me! Moping about at home won't do me much good and I don't feel I'll be much use in the office for a while. Please? You can always get someone else later, if it doesn't work out.'

Melissa looked up at him. Her eyes shone with the intensity of her feelings. Her face looked more like her usual animated self. How could he refuse!

'All right! I'll give you chance, but it will have to satisfy the full board.'

'I'll give my all,' she assured him.

The waiter removed their starter plates and soon returned with the next course, seasonal melon for Melissa and deep-fried whitebait for Trent.

'Will you be able to give me a list of the wines to be included and their prices?' Melissa asked. 'Also, I'll need some information about the various areas where the wines come from. I expect there are reference books about it all, and photographs.'

'You will have heard a lot about what you need to know at the international conference you were at in Marseille. Have you brought my notes back?'

Melissa frowned with concentration.

'There was a folder in my flight bag. I haven't looked at it yet. I've been too concerned with my personal problems. Do you think that could be it?'

'Probably.'

He thought briefly of the telephone conversation he had had with one of the other delegates, who wondered if Melissa had been taken ill in the second week of conference, as she hadn't made many appearances, but he decided not to mention it. He looked again at her eager expression and smiled at her.

His heart missed a beat. She looked so lovely! He felt new stirrings of desire for her. Yet, look what had happened before! She had become more and more possessive and demanding, almost killing his love for her. Could he take that risk again?

5

On their arrival at work the following day, Melissa finally had her tour around the whole building, briefly meeting most of the other employees. She was aware of their mild curiosity about her but everyone seemed prepared to accept her as she now was.

Trent suggested that she worked in the library so that the bustle and constant interruptions wouldn't disturb her creative flow. She enjoyed the solitude and many reference books were there at hand.

However, she missed the chatter and made sure she took her breaks at the same time as at least one of the office girls, thus keeping up her relationship with them. Now that she was no longer in their department, even Lauren seemed happy enough to let bygones be bygones and Melissa threw herself wholeheartedly into researching the added information she needed for the new brochure.

She retyped the list of wines and current prices and searched through various travel brochures to discover local conditions of the regions where the grapes were grown. She felt drawn to certain areas of Italy, feeling a sort of kinship with the region. She was also aware of the growing depth of her feelings towards Trent. He was always busy at work, some days travelling to meet clients but he usually found time to pop into the library a couple of times a day and she could sense a softening in the attention he paid her.

He was kind and caring and, at times, she was also aware of a smouldering desire in his eyes, but, at other times, Trent seemed to step back from her. Was that out of respect for her memory loss? Or was it because he had reservations about renewing their relationship? Maybe he was as confused as she was. She knew her reactions weren't always consistent and, tying in with Lauren and the others, she had changed since her accident. Was Trent disappointed in her in some way?

She was obviously much quieter and more reserved than before. Did Trent prefer a social butterfly? She considered livening herself up, but felt it would be dishonest to pretend.

During the Friday afternoon tea break at the end of the first week, Lauren was in the rest room at the same time as Melissa. As Lauren rose to leave, she remarked that she and Nicola and Emma were going to a nightclub that evening to celebrate her birthday and invited Melissa to join them.

'That's very thoughtful of you,' Melissa responded, touched by the girl's show of friendliness. 'I'd love to, but I'd better check with Trent first, in case he has something planned.'

'Don't let the man in your life rule over you!' Lauren warned. 'They don't think we can enjoy ourselves without them. Besides, it's a girls' night out.

We'll find our own men, thank you very much!'

She spoke lightly and Melissa laughed with her.

'I'll check with him, just in case and let you know before we go home.'

'Cool! You'll enjoy it. You're quite a party chick once you get going!'

Melissa doubted that would be the case but found herself looking forward to it, and something from her former lifestyle might click into place.

Trent was a little dubious when she told him of the invitation.

'Are you sure you're up to it? These events can get pretty wild if you don't know what to expect, and you might not know anyone else.'

'I'll be fine,' she assured him. 'I'll be with Lauren, Emma and Nicola, and I won't stay too late.'

She chose a pair of fitted, shiny black pants and a short-cropped white lacy top to wear. Trent insisted on dropping her off at the chosen meeting point. He then drove off to meet with some of his own friends at another venue. Lauren and Emma were already there and Nicola arrived soon after. Melissa had bought a bottle of perfume for Lauren, having discovered her favourite fragrance and she handed it over with a birthday greeting. The four girls chatted animatedly for a while and then Nicola stood up.

'Come on. We're going to Bondini's now. We've booked a table for nine-thirty and then we're off to The Cabaret to dance until we drop!'

It was a whirlwind of an evening. Melissa felt herself to be on the outside of the group for the greater part of the time, but the others kept bringing her into the conversations, reminding her of other evenings out they had had together. She was enjoying their company and had no qualms about continuing on to the nightclub.

Bright lights arced and dazzled around the dimmed interior. Music blared and the place was a crush of partying people. The four girls kept together at first, dancing in a group on the crowded dance floor. Melissa hadn't noticed them being split up until she realised that she couldn't see any of the others. She wasn't worried. Eventually, she saw Nicola and waved at her. It didn't seem to matter whether you had a partner or not and Melissa continued to dance until she felt in need of a drink. She had just ordered a glass of white wine when someone gripped her upper arm tightly.

'Melissa! I'm surprised to see you here again! Took the hint, did you?'

It was a tall, lean-faced young man, dressed all in black. His expression was most unpleasant.

'Sorry to hear of your accident. It's spoiled your pretty face a bit, eh?'

Melissa felt at an immediate disadvantage. She didn't know him and she instinctively disliked him. She didn't feel inclined to tell him about her temporary loss of memory and tried to bluff it out.

'I don't know what you mean,' she

said lightly. 'Why shouldn't I come here with my friends?'

'Yeah, well, anything can happen to change one's mind, can't it?'

'Such as?'

'Such as not intending to pay up! If that's your intention, you're playing a dangerous game, baby!'

Pay up? What did he mean? Her unuttered question was interrupted by Lauren grabbing hold of her arm.

'Come along to the little girls' room, Melissa. I've got a packet. Sorry, Lenny. You're too late!'

She dragged a bewildered Melissa through the dancers on the floor to a darkened corridor that led to the ladies' room.

'You don't buy from Lenny, do you? He's a rip-off!'

She made a swift inspection of the six cubicles, satisfying herself that they were all empty.

'What are we doing?' Melissa asked, puzzled by Lauren's antics.

Lauren pushed her inside the first

cubicle and closed the door.

'Lauren!' Melissa said sharply. 'I don't know what you're up to but I'm not being a party to it. Let me out!'

'Don't be a spoilsport! You love this! Here!'

She handed Melissa a cigarette, closed down the toilet seat and climbed up on to the low cistern, where she seated herself and calmly began to light her cigarette.

'Sit down and light yours,' she invited.

'I don't smoke,' Melissa denied, 'and even if I did, I wouldn't smoke it in here like this. I may have lost my memory but I'm not stupid.'

Lauren's cigarette had a strange smell to it. Melissa instinctively disliked it. She thrust her unused cigarette back at Lauren.

'Here! I don't want it! You'd better have it back.'

'Loosen up, Melissa! You're usually quite a raver when you get going!'

The smell from Lauren's cigarette

was making Melissa feel light-headed.

'I'm going,' she declared and struggled to open the door.

'Don't you dare tell anyone!' Lauren threatened. 'I'll know it's you, if there's any bother!'

'What you do in your own time is nothing to do with me,' Melissa replied. 'I'll see you on Monday.'

She made her way back to the dance floor. Lauren was smoking pot! Did Nicola and Emma do drugs as well? And had Lauren spoken the truth when she had said that she did? She felt bewildered. How had she decided Lauren was smoking pot when she couldn't even remember her own past? How far was she implicated in it? And what about that man at the bar? Lenny, Lauren had called him. She didn't want to bump into him again.

She kept to the edge of the dance floor and carefully skirted her way around it, searching the dancers for a sight of Emma or Nicola. Ah, there was Nicola! She waved to her. Nicola made her way over, dragging her partner with her.

'Hi, Melissa! This is Tim. Are you having a good time?'

'Hi, Tim. Yes, sort of, but I think I'll go now. Is that all right with you?'

'Yes, sure. Will you ring Trent?'

'Yes. I've got my phone. Tell Emma I've gone, won't you?'

She collected her jacket from the cloakroom and slipped out into the street. She stayed within the cover of the doorway and took out her phone. She hoped he wouldn't mind his evening being cut short. As she waited for him to answer, she glanced at her watch. It was ten past one! She couldn't believe it! Time had flown!

'Trent Gresham speaking,' his familiar voice spoke in her ear.

'Trent? I'm sorry! I didn't realise how late it was!'

'You really are the limit, Melissa! I've been out of my mind with worry!'

'I'm sorry. Shall I call a taxi?'

'No! I'll come! Where are you?'

His voice sounded a bit terse. She couldn't blame him, it was so late! She looked around, wondering what the street name was.

'I'm . . . er . . . '

The neon sign hanging down from the wall caught her eye.

'I'm at The Cabaret,' she told him.

'Wait there! I'll be right with you!'

The phone went dead in her hand so she switched it off and replaced it in her bag. Before she had straightened up, an arm grabbed hold of her.

It was Lenny again, and two others.

'You weren't thinking of leaving, were you? We haven't concluded our business yet!'

Melissa tried to shake her arm free but Lenny held it too tightly.

'Let go of me! I don't know who you are and I've certainly never done any business with you!'

'Ha! Listen to the little lady! Cut out the comedy business and listen carefully! This is your last warning! Pay up, or else I won't hold myself responsible for what happens to you! It won't be a near miss like last time! These friends of mine enjoy making people wish they'd paid their debts a little sooner!'

Melissa drew in her breath sharply. Was Lenny responsible for her accident, or was he just making use of it to frighten her? Whichever, she believed his threat. They looked a nasty pair. She looked back at Lenny.

'How much do I owe you?' she asked fearfully.

'That's more like it, girlie! See what effect you have on her, boys? One look at you and she's willing to pay up!'

He turned back to Melissa, thrusting his face into hers.

'Let's call it two thousand pounds, with a hundred pounds a day on top until you pay it! So, the sooner you pay, the less it will be!'

Melissa felt the blood drain from her face.

'Two thousand pounds! I haven't got that amount of money!'

'No? Then you'd better start finding

some quickly, hadn't you? Here, give the lady a taste of what she'll get!'

He flung her backwards towards the two other men. She felt herself falling as one of the men grabbed hold of her and twisted her arms up her back. The other stood in front of her, leering into her face. Melissa recoiled in terror. What was he going to do?

She realised he had a knife in his hand and jerked backwards as he held it towards her face. Her eyes were wide with terror. The man grinned, delighting in her fright. He touched the point of his knife to her face just in front of her right ear.

'Pity to spoil your lovely face, isn't it, girlie!'

She felt the point of the knife pierce her skin and she screamed, kicking out at his shins. The man just laughed and drew the knife downwards. It felt like a searing hot line of fire. As she screamed again, she was aware of a car speeding along the road. It screeched to a standstill and a man leaped out. The three men holding her thrust her at the figure as he ran round his car and leaped towards them. They then dispersed at a run in three directions.

Melissa sank against her rescuer. She knew it was Trent, even though she hadn't seen his face. Her legs were shaking and her whole body trembling.

He held her tight, murmuring, 'It's all right! It's all right!'

But it wasn't! How could it be? She somehow owed those men two thousand pounds. How was she to tell Trent?

'Get in the car!' Trent commanded her harshly.

He propelled her across the pavement and yanked open the passenger door. She bent down and he half-guided, half-pushed her into the passenger seat and slammed the door shut. Within a minute, he was in the driving seat and fastening his seatbelt.

'Fasten your belt!'

His voice sounded cold, but Melissa did as she was told, though her hands were trembling. Her mind was in turmoil. These things didn't happen to ordinary people! They were things you read about in the newspapers.

'I'm sorry, Trent. I don't know what it was all about! The man just leaped on to me. I was terrified! I thought he was going to kill me!'

He glanced sideways at her and the bleakness in his eyes made Melissa shrink away from him.

'I suppose you've been up to your old tricks again, haven't you?'

His voice was cold, his tone defeated. From what she had learned during the evening, she was somehow involved in taking drugs and she felt very apprehensive about just how far her involvement went.

Melissa was shocked by Trent's accusation, the tone it was uttered in, and by the possibility that it might be justified! She leaned against her seat in silence, her mind vainly struggling to sort out the confusing thoughts.

No-one was on duty at Crompton

Court and Trent drove the car into the underground garage himself.

'Out!' he said abruptly.

The single word command was worse than a tirade of accusations. She opened her door and weakly climbed out of the car. She felt dizzy and leaned against the car for support.

'Had too much to drink, as well?' Trent queried tonelessly.

'No, I don't think so.'

'Short-term memory gone as well, now, has it?'

'No,' she replied in an equally cold voice. 'Do you treat all victims of muggings in this peremptory manner?'

'Some victims have gone looking for trouble!'

'Meaning?'

'Don't make a scene here, Melissa! It will be recorded by the security camera and I don't want to go through all that again!'

Melissa considered his words, especially the last one. She hadn't been going to make a scene, but Trent obviously expected one. Did she often make scenes? She marched silently ahead of him as he guided her in the direction of the internal exit from the garage. He pressed the security button and gave his name and flat number. The lift door slid open and they rode up to the first floor in silence.

The stony atmosphere continued into the flat. A flicker of concern betrayed his finer feelings. He held her chin and twisted her head round slightly to her right, so that he could look at it more closely.

'A scratch!' he diagnosed tersely. 'Wash it well with hot water before you go to bed. I'll see you in the morning.'

'Is that all you are going to say?'

He turned and looked at her wearily.

'What else is there to say?'

'Plenty! You obviously know more about this than I do! Who were those men, and what did they mean?'

He sighed wearily again.

'What did they say?'

'That I owe them two thousand pounds.'

'Right! I'll pay them tomorrow. Now, may I go to bed?'

'Is that all you're going to say?'

'What else do you want?'

'Answers! Such as who are they? How do I know them? What have I bought off them?'

Reluctantly, she admitted to herself that she knew the answer to the final question, if not the previous two.

'They are drug merchants. You have met them in the various nightclubs you frequent, and you probably owe the money for drugs.'

Melissa was stunned. She had begun to suspect what he was saying, but to hear it put so calmly and bluntly, completely bowled her over. She felt her antipathy towards him shrivel away.

'Perfectly clear, thank you. I will see you in the morning.'

With her head held high, she swung about on her heel and strode into her bedroom, making sure she closed the door quietly. She'd leave the slamming of doors routine to Melissa! She stopped dead in her tracks. She was Melissa, wasn't she? She stared quietly at the closed door. Was she going out of her mind?

She didn't sleep well. Her confused thoughts tumbled over and over themselves. Why did she sometimes feel as though she was on the outside of herself, looking in?

Trent rose early, long before her. There was the appetising smell of toast and coffee drifting from the kitchen. She joined him hesitantly.

'Good morning. Did you sleep well?' he asked with enforced gaiety.

'Not really,' she replied as she slid on to a stool. 'Did you?'

'No. I didn't expect to.'

Melissa took a slice of toast and began to spread a little butter on it.

'Trent?'

'Yes?'

'I know you're angry with me, but I don't completely know why. I didn't know where we were going to end up last night, and, even if I had, it wouldn't have meant anything to me. I don't remember ever being there before, though I'm sure you're about to tell me otherwise!'

'Yes. It's one of your favourite haunts, though there are others!'

'So? I like going to nightclubs! I can't say I really enjoyed it there last night but I expect it will grow on me, with practice!'

'Melissa, it's not so much the nightclub, but what goes on there! Do you get my meaning?'

She was beginning to, but she needed him to spell it out.

'Tell me!'

'All right! You have been buying drugs from those men. From what he implied last night, you have been having them on tick, presumably to sell on to other addicts. Now, do you understand?'

Melissa was horrified.

'You mean I'm a pusher?'

'I don't know, Melissa. I never thought so, but why else do you owe the man two thousand pounds?'

'I don't know! I just don't know!'

She dropped her head into her hands. It was worse than she had feared. It was bad enough to be taking drugs, but to be pushing them as well! What else did she get up to? She felt Trent's hand on her shoulder.

'It mightn't be that bad. There might be another explanation but . . . '

'You can't think of one?'

'Not off-hand, no.'

'I must be an awful person!'

'No, Melissa. Maybe you've been a bit naïve, but you're not awful.'

'But it's illegal, isn't it? I could go to prison!'

'It isn't that bad, yet! We don't know what it's all about. The man might be just blackmailing you or something!'

'Blackmailing me? What about?'

'I don't know! Maybe just because he knows you've taken drugs and he's trying to make a big deal out of it.'

'I don't feel like I take drugs.'

'You told me you'd given them up. It was just before we met. You had begun to act unpredictably but I didn't suspect you were back on drugs.'

'So, what shall I do?' she asked desperately.

'What do you think?'

Melissa had lain awake most of the night reaching her decision.

'I think I should go to the police and tell them as much as I know,' she said slowly but with conviction. 'Otherwise, Lenny is going to be on my back for ever. And I need to leave here. No! Don't try to dissuade me! I've made up my mind. I can't have your name dragged down with my own! I'll start to pack my things.'

'No, no, Melissa! You can't go! I'm falling in love with you all over again! We'll face this thing together.'

He crushed her to him and his lips found hers. Melissa felt her body melt into his. Time stood still until her head swam with an incredible joy. When

Trent finally raised his head and smiled into her eyes, Melissa lost all her fear of what might happen. It wouldn't matter. Trent loved her as much as she loved him.

Intermingling more kissing with discussing what to do for the best, Trent finally made the decision.

'I'm going to get in touch with a good lawyer I know. We need advice from someone who is more familiar with these things than ourselves, but it will probably involve a fresh assessment of your present mental condition. Do you have any problems with that?'

'No.'

She had been going to request a check-up. She would be able to ask about her confusion about a double identity.

Trent telephoned both the hospital and his lawyer. The contact at the hospital made an appointment for Monday morning, as a follow-up visit after her discharge the previous week.

Monday afternoon was arranged with the lawyer. Melissa felt much happier with herself and, when Trent mentioned that it was his mother's birthday the following day, she willingly agreed to accompany him on a birthday visit.

'Have I met them before?' she asked warily.

'Yes, but only occasionally, usually on a Sunday afternoon. It's over a month since you last went.'

'Do they like me?'

'Of course. A friend of mine is a friend of mother's.'

Melissa wasn't convinced of that but didn't say so.

The weather was warm and sunny on the Sunday. Their bronzed arms touched as Trent changed gear, sending a warm thrill down Melissa's arm. She wondered if he felt it, too. They were soon on the edge of the moors and Melissa sighed in contentment.

'It's lovely up here, isn't it? I'd like to live in a place like this. It's near enough to Manchester to be handy for work, but also on the edge of untamed countryside.'

'You didn't used to feel that. Too many muddy fields was your previous censure.'

'Was it?'

She mused on the subject. It really unsettled her. She was looking forward to being able to discuss it with the doctor on Monday.

Mr and Mrs Gresham lived in a large, detached house, stone-built and set in its own grounds. Mrs Gresham opened the door and welcomed them both inside. She was quite tall, aged about fifty, Melissa guessed. She was an attractive woman with loose dark, curly hair framing her face. She received Trent's hug, kiss and birthday greeting with a fond smile and then held out her arms to Melissa.

'It's lovely to see you again, Melissa. We were so sorry to hear about your accident. Now, make yourself at home and don't worry about a thing. If we ask you something you can't remember, blame us for forgetting!'

Melissa liked her instantly.

'Thank you, Mrs Gresham. Trent has been very supportive to me, also. I do appreciate it. And happy birthday! We've brought you these flowers and Trent has a gift to give you later.'

'Thank you. They're lovely. I must put them in some water straight away. And you must call me Sheila, dear. Mrs Gresham sounds far too formal. Now, what would you like to drink? A glass of wine, perhaps?'

'That would be lovely.'

'Good. Jim is just through there. Take her through, Trent, while I attend to these flowers.'

Jim Gresham was just as nice. He also was tall, though more stockily built than his son.

'Welcome back, Melissa. You're still as pretty as a picture!'

Glass of wine in hand, they sauntered out into the huge, rear garden where a number of people were conversing in small groups.

'Don't worry. You've not met anyone else before,' Trent whispered in her ear, 'and only Lisa, my sister, and her husband, Simon, know about your accident.'

Melissa was glad about that. She could just be herself, without wondering if she were living up to her former character. Lisa and Simon were friendly and asked her mainly about the brochure she was creating. She soon became confident enough to approach others and enjoyed the light-hearted conversations with them.

Lunch was served as a buffet with everyone helping themselves and sitting anywhere they wished. Trent produced a camera.

'It's yours,' he told Melissa. 'I noticed you've only got four shots left so I thought we may as well use them up. You never know, your holiday snaps may revive a few memories.'

He took a couple of shots and someone took one of him and Melissa and the last one of Sheila and Jim.

'We'll pop them in the chemist's tomorrow on our way to the hospital.'

It was an altogether lovely day and Melissa was pleased to have coped so well. She felt better able to face her check-up on Monday.

She was relieved when Trent announced that he was to accompany her. Mr Hughes soon put her at ease and, with gentle questioning, persuaded her to talk about what she could remember and how she felt at various times. He nodded when she spoke about feeling as though she was on the outside, looking in at herself.

'Did you bring the photographs?' he asked Trent.

Trent nodded.

'Yes, they're here.'

He turned aside to Melissa.

'They're from a skiing holiday we spent together in February.'

'I want you to speak out your thoughts as you see them,' Mr Hughes explained. 'Try not to think before you speak. I want your first reaction.'

The snaps were mainly taken on the ski slopes, with a number of people dressed in colourful ski-suits, skiing or posing. She could pick out Trent and, sometimes, herself. They were wearing hats and goggles but she'd seen her red ski-suit in her wardrobe at home. Towards the end there was a close-up of her laughing face, caught completely unposed. She laughed.

'That's a good one of Melissa!' She paused. 'I've done it again, haven't I? You see what I mean?'

Mr Hughes nodded slowly. He leaned forward, his elbows on the table.

'Yes, I do. I can't be one hundred per cent sure at this stage, but it seems to me that you could be suffering from a temporary, I hope, case of mild schizophrenia.'

She looked at Trent to gauge his reaction. Like her, he seemed startled. She turned back to the doctor.

'Isn't that quite serious?'

'It can be, but, in your case, as I said, I hope it is only temporary. I can prescribe some drugs for you to take that might help to restore the chemical imbalance in your body, but I think I would rather wait a while and hope your body starts to cure itself. We are, as it says in one of the psalms, fearfully and wonderfully made. Our bodies can often restore such imbalances that I think you may be suffering from. How do you feel about that?'

Melissa looked to Trent for support. He squeezed her hand comfortingly.

'We'll face it together,' he promised.

Melissa turned back to Mr Hughes and nodded.

'I'll do whatever you think best. Am I likely to get worse?'

Mr Hughes smiled benignly.

'In some cases it is a progressive condition, but I have every hope that you will recover. It's early days yet, just about two weeks since the accident, isn't it? Come and see me again in two weeks time, earlier if you feel the need. I'll give you my private card in case you need it.'

They made the visit to Trent's lawyer in the afternoon, a man named Roger Peterson. He listened carefully to Melissa's story, making copious notes. His advice was to wait until they knew more about Melissa's condition and to try to determine just what the two thousand pounds was for.

'I'll represent you in the matter,' he said to Melissa. 'I've heard of the man and it's more likely to be some sort of scam than a genuine debt. I know the lawyer who usually represents him. I'll get in touch with him, Trent, and we'll take it from there.'

Melissa spent a better night. At least her problems were out in the open.

When her holiday snaps were collected the following day, however, all other questions were pushed to the background. Featuring on most of the snaps was the smiling, suntanned image of a very good-looking young man, his arm resting possessively round Melissa's shoulders.

6

'Who is that?' Trent asked, his voice sounding casual but Melissa could tell that his intention was anything but!

She stared at the photographs in dismay.

'I don't know.'

Her heart sank. The fact that she didn't know the man had very little to do with the question. It was more a question of why were they in such an intimate pose?

'I'm sorry, Trent. I seem to have behaved badly. What can I say?'

Trent stared grimly at the two smiling faces on the photograph.

'It's no use pretending I'm not upset by it, Melissa. I am. No wonder you stayed an extra week. It's a pity you can't enlarge on it. Have you no memory of him at all?'

'None at all. It's as if I've never seen

him before, but the photographs prove that I have. I'm sorry.'

She felt terrible. Whether it had been a light-hearted holiday romance or something more serious, she had no idea. She looked relaxed and happy on the photographs. She had betrayed Trent's trust of her.

They were sitting on the sofa, supposedly sharing a happy reminiscence of Melissa's trip to France, hoping the snapshots would trigger some memory chords. Instead, they had revealed her fickleness. Trent took hold of both of her hands, gently and tenderly, to Melissa's surprise.

'How do you feel when you look at the photographs?' he asked.

'Bewildered,' she replied honestly. 'I can't imagine why I did this. I care too much about you! I must have been out of my mind!'

'I suppose I should draw comfort from the fact that you left him behind and came back to me,' Trent said with forced lightness. 'As long as you aren't planning to rush back to him?'

'I wouldn't even know where to find him, and I certainly don't want to!'

She studied the photograph again, looking in vain for some hint that they were just part of a group relaxing together.

'Why was I on holiday without you?' she asked Trent. 'Had we had a row or something?'

'No, not really, and, regardless of how it appears from those snaps, you weren't there on holiday. You were attending an international convention of wine merchants, supposedly searching out new business and extending your own contacts.'

'I seem to have done that!' she said ruefully. 'The latter part, anyway.'

She was immediately contrite for her light-heartedness.

'I'm sorry. It's no joking matter. What do you want me to do? Do you want me to leave?'

'No, of course not. I think we should keep the arrangement as it is. You might recover your memory and remember that you came back to finish with me!'

Melissa doubted that very much! She had fallen very much in love with him and just wanted the nightmare to be over.

Melissa felt very much on edge the next few days. It wasn't anything that Trent said or did. He couldn't have been kinder. He spoke affectionately to her and was very supportive, but she wished he would take her into his arms and hold her close. She wanted such a lot, but deserved none of it.

The next few days were difficult. It was a strain to be living so closely with Trent but feeling herself a million miles away from him. Her worries seemed to press down heavily upon her. She wondered if the depression she felt was part of the schizophrenia.

Her time at work was the only time she felt completely relaxed. At least, whilst there, she could forget her problems for a while. The brochure was coming along nicely. She had sorted out the pictures she wanted to use and had nearly finished the final draft of the blurbs about each wine they were advertising.

Trent had introduced her to wine tasting, showing her how to enjoy the visual aspect of the wine in the glass, then to inhale the aroma, and lastly, to take a little of the wine into her mouth and let its individual flavour imprint itself in her memory before delicately spitting it into a receptacle. She revelled in the intimacy of the occupation, relieved that they could both behave with professionalism, putting their personal relationship aside.

It was strange, she thought. She now felt she could identify over twenty different wines and remember all their characteristics, but she couldn't remember . . . she nearly said another name but that was ridiculous. She was Melissa Fielding. But she only knew that because that was what she had been told. She wanted to know it, really know it.

Sometimes she felt she was on the verge of remembering, but when she tried to reach out to take hold of it, it hovered just out of reach, or faded away altogether.

One time, it was her parents. She longed to remember them. Thankfully, the memories that drifted on the edge of her consciousness were happy ones. They must have been wonderful parents. And she was sure she had had a sister, or was that her dual personality? She felt happier in the quieter character but, somewhere nearby, a bewitching sprite danced lightly.

One evening, Trent looked up from the newspaper he was reading.

'There's a food and drink programme on television tonight that should interest you. It's taking a look at the vineyards of Italy. We get some of our wines from one of the vineyards mentioned. You probably met some of their representatives in Marseille. You might recognise him or her.'

The programme started with an

overview of the whole region — small townships nestling amongst the lower slopes of mountains, whitewashed villas basking in the sunshine and vast acres of green vineyards.

'It's lovely there,' Melissa breathed in contentment. 'There's a river and a delightful restaurant on the terraces. Look! There it is!'

It was indeed an attractive setting. The olive-skinned restaurant owner was being interviewed. His face beamed and his arms waved volubly as he described life in the village and his own particular rôle there. Melissa laughed and echoed his sentiments, seconds before the translation began.

'You speak Italian!' Trent said in surprise. 'You've never said.'

'Do I? I mean, haven't I?'

Melissa considered the point. The voiced-over conversation was still proceeding.

'Yes, I suppose I do. Oh, I know her!'

She pointed to the screen. A large society wedding was being filmed. The bride and groom, a handsome couple in their fifties, were mingling with their guests. Melissa grasped hold of Trent's arm, her face alight with recognition.

'It's . . . '

The name wouldn't come. Melissa furrowed her brow in frustration.

'I was at that wedding!' she declared firmly.

'You couldn't have been there!' Trent contradicted her. 'It was early in July. You were here in England.'

'But . . . '

Melissa paused. The news clip seemed so familiar to her. She felt she knew what was just off screen and when the camera moved across the scene, her anticipation was proved correct. Suddenly, she saw her own image. She was standing just behind the happy couple, a glass of wine in her hand, chatting to a corpulent Italian.

'See! I'm there!' she exclaimed, grabbing hold of Trent's arm. 'Look! Just . . . oh, you've missed it! It was me! I know it was!'

She looked at Trent's face. He looked uncertain, wanting to believe her but without evidence, how could he? She bit her lip. Had she seen only what she wanted to see? Yet her face had looked so real.

'Am I going out of my mind?' she asked in despair.

Trent laid his hand on hers and patted it.

'No, of course not!' he hastened to assure her. 'It's still early days after your accident. You are probably beginning to remember some things and are still confused about others.'

'It's like being in a thick mist that the wind blows away for a fleeting moment and then it comes sweeping in again. I wish it would lift off me completely!'

'It will. Set your sights on the future. The present can take care of itself.'

Melissa shook her head. His words didn't really help.

'How can I look forward to the future when I can't remember my past?'

Trent remained awake long after he

had gone to bed. Melissa had been so sure that she had been at that wedding, but how could she have been?

Once Melissa had retired to her room, he had checked the dates in his diary and she had definitely been here in England. It had been the weekend of that disastrous last visit to his parents' home, the occasion that had made him seriously consider whether or not their relationship had any future. He was glad he hadn't ended it there and then. He was now seeing a much gentler side to Melissa, but he couldn't help worrying about the way she imagined she had been somewhere else.

Mr Hughes had drawn him aside after the consultation at the hospital and warned him of the serious nature of schizophrenia. Though he hoped that Melissa was suffering from a temporary attack, it was generally a progressive condition that could have disastrous effects on relationships within even the closest of families. Mr Hughes had warned him to weigh the situation carefully before he took their relation-ship further, but how could he desert her now, at a time when she needed him most?

It wasn't as though she had any family to care about her, and she was different since she had returned from France, less volatile and unpredictable, more caring and considerate. He had meant it when he had said he was falling in love with her all over again, and he wasn't about to turn his back on her.

Just before he fell asleep, an idea came to him. Why hadn't he thought of it earlier? Rafaele Bonelli, his main contact in the Italian wine trade, would possibly know whose wedding had been filmed as part of the promotional video. He was sure he could make a discreet enquiry without betraying any confi-dences and he would take it from there.

The phone call went better than he had hoped. Rafaele was only too pleased to speak of his friendship with Cesare Galliano and his beautiful bride, the renowned fashion designer, Fabia Romayne. Yes, he knew them well. Had Trent not seen him in the film of the grand wedding reception?

Trent admitted that regretfully he hadn't.

'There is a matter I would very much like to discuss with Senor Galliano, Rafaele. Do you think you could discover his private telephone number and address for me?'

Rafaele returned his call within five minutes and gave Trent the required information. Trent thanked him and, after a few more mundane remarks, drew the conversation to a close. He sat quietly for a moment or two, looking thoughtfully at the telephone.

He absentmindedly tapped the end of his pen on the polished top of his desk. He knew what he intended to do but he wasn't sure that he should do it. Would he be acting in an underhand manner? Would Melissa be upset if she knew about the enquiries he was making? Maybe the old Melissa would have been, but he now believed she would look upon it differently. It was for her sake he was doing it. If it came to nothing, she need never know.

He reached out his right hand to pick up the computer mouse and activated his screen. Then, with well-practised movements, he clicked on to the Internet and booked himself a return flight to Rome.

7

Melissa was a bit taken aback when Trent told her that he was going on a business trip abroad for a few days. She couldn't visualise life without him and it scared her.

'Where are you going?' she asked.

Trent avoided making eye contact. Melissa sensed he was ill at ease.

'I'm . . . er . . . meeting with one of our local contacts at one of the vineyards from which we purchase a rather large consignment of wine,' he said somewhat too nonchalantly to ring completely true.

Melissa felt unable to press it any further. She felt that he didn't trust her for some reason and could only suppose that her disloyalty whilst on holiday had made him wary of taking her into his confidence.

'Will you be away long?' she went on.

'I shouldn't think so. A couple of days or so. If you need anything in my absence, get in touch with Roger Peterson. I'm sorry I'm rushing off like this but the circumstance only cropped up late last night. Roger is sorting out that business with Lenny. He has demanded a full statement of the debt and a signed receipt for the money, then there'll be no recurrence of any demands on you.'

He took a step towards her. Melissa wondered if he was going to take her in his arms. She wanted him to. She wanted to feel the strength of his body supporting her, but he drew back.

'Do you feel all right about going into the office on your own?' he asked almost diffidently.

A lump in her throat prevented her answering straight away. She nodded.

'I'll take a taxi. I don't think I'd know how to get there on my own.'

'Great! Well, that's it for now. I've left a message on the answer phone at work, so my absence will be no surprise there. Take care.'

He did move forward and kiss her, but only briefly, barely touching her lips at all. And then he was gone.

Melissa felt dreadfully alone. Trent was her anchor in life. He was the only fact she felt sure about. With him away, she felt vulnerable. Her only other shelter was the office.

She spent the whole day finalising the brochure, breaking off only to have a hasty tea break and a sandwich for her lunch. Lauren was in the dining-room. Melissa halted, remembering Friday night. Lauren, too, seemed unsure about how to greet Melissa. Not being one to carry grudges, Melissa smiled at her.

'Hi, Lauren!'

Lauren grimaced ruefully.

'Hi, yourself! Er, sorry about Friday. I shouldn't have pressed you to . . . er, you know what,' she added quietly, looking around guiltily to make sure no-one could overhear. 'Emma said you left early. Did Lenny find you? He said he was looking for you.'

'Yes. He wasn't very nice!'

'He never is. It's not wise to get on the wrong side of him. He doesn't give any quarter, but you'd know all about that!'

'That's just it, Lauren, I don't know!'

She paused, wondering whether or not it would be wise to confide in Lauren. She decided she had nothing to lose.

'What sort of hold has Lenny got over me?'

Lauren's eyes opened wide.

'Have you really forgotten so completely? It's weird!'

'Tell me about it! I'm a bit scared of him, but I don't know why.'

'Everyone's scared of Lenny. The thing is, he never lets go. You'd be as well to pay up and hope he'll leave you alone. Does Trent know about it?'

'He knows as much as I do, which isn't much at all.'

Something niggled at the back of her mind, something she should have told

Trent. It wouldn't come.

'Why do I owe him so much money? Was it for drugs?'

Lauren shook her head.

'I don't know. It could have been. You didn't confide in any of us. Like I said, pay up and then keep out of his way. You should be all right, with Trent Gresham being your boyfriend.'

Melissa couldn't help feeling uneasy as she returned to the library. Trent had left the matter in Roger Peterson's hands, but what if Lenny wasn't content to accept that? What would he do? Would he try to see her again?

By the end of normal working hours, Melissa had only a few more changes to make to the final draft of the brochure, so she stayed behind a bit later than usual to run off a first copy so that she could take it home to study it carefully. It was surprising how many mistakes undetected on the computer screen seemed to leap out in bold ink once it was printed and she wanted to make sure she had spotted them all.

She finally leaned back in her chair in satisfaction, her hands clasped behind her head as she watched the printed pages slide out of the printer. She stretched her neck and rolled her shoulders backwards a few times. That felt better! There was only the cleaning staff still around when she finally left. She rang for a taxi and went down to the foyer to wait for it.

A car appeared around the far corner of the street and pulled into the kerb. Melissa stepped towards it, realising too late that it wasn't the expected taxi. She drew back with an apologetic smile at the driver, turning back towards the building. She didn't see the man who leaped out of the car. The first she knew was when both of her arms were grabbed from behind. Before she could call out or try to break free, she was dragged towards the car and bundled unceremoniously on to the back seat. The man squashed in on top of her and the car immediately sped away.

Melissa felt as though her breath had

been forced out of her lungs. She fought to draw in deep gulps of air. This couldn't be happening! But it was. She screamed. Immediately, her face was pressed into the soft fabric of the seat cover. Panic seized hold of her. She couldn't breathe. She managed to turn her face slightly and gasped in some air. Though thoroughly frightened, she made herself relax and felt the firm grip of her captor's hand relax also.

She managed to lift her face away from the upholstery of the seat and twisted her head round. She didn't know the man but thought he was possibly one of the men with Lenny last Friday.

'Where are you taking me?'

'You'll find out soon enough.'

'I haven't any money on me. It's being dealt with by my solicitor.'

'Lenny doesn't deal with solicitors.'

'Well, he'll have to deal with mine!' Melissa snapped with a bravado she didn't feel.

It was perfectly true that she didn't

have any money. She apparently sailed very close to the wind. The only money in her bank account was her first month's salary that Trent had arranged to be paid in advance when he had accompanied her to the bank to stand surety for her changing her pin number.

A cold shudder suddenly ran through her. Now she remembered what she hadn't told Trent! Lenny had implied on Friday night that he was responsible for the hit-and-run accident! And Lauren had said he was a dangerous man to cross! What did he plan to do with her?

'You're not going to believe this!' the driver remarked over his shoulder to the man at her side. 'I'm going to have to stop somewhere for petrol. Lenny'll go mad if he finds out!'

'There's a garage half a mile down the road. We'd best call in there, and you keep your head down!' the man added, digging Melissa in her back.

Melissa remained quiet. It might give her an opportunity to escape, or at least to be caught on a security camera. She waited until the driver had left the car and was putting petrol into the tank.

'I need to use the toilet,' she demanded.

'Tough!'

'I'm not joking! You've given me quite a fright and I always react like this when I'm nervous. I can't hold out much longer!'

'There are no toilets here, anyway! It's only a garage.'

'All garages have toilets!'

'Well, you'd better not try anything! I'll be right behind you!'

He allowed Melissa to struggle into a sitting position and then pressed the button to let down the window.

'She says she needs the loo. What d'you reckon?'

Melissa didn't hear the reply, but it must have been favourable because the man slid out of his seat and pulled her out after him.

'No tricks, now! Lenny'll only track you down again. He wants to talk to you, that's all! It may as well be today as tomorrow!'

That was his opinion! Melissa wasn't prepared to verify it. She tossed back her head and strode ahead of him into the shop, smiling brightly at the young attendant.

'I know I'm a nuisance, but could I possibly use your loo?'

'It's outside, round the back.'

'Thanks. You're an angel!'

She looked up at the security camera, just in case she didn't manage to escape, amazed at her cool reaction. She supposed she was in shock and the terror of it would hit her later.

Her heart sank when she saw the small room. It was in a line of storerooms set at a right angle to the main building. The door had only a latch and a small bolt. She went inside and slid the bolt into place. There was a high, small window, too small to allow an easy exit, although it was swinging loose.

Set behind the outer door, on the

adjacent wall, was another door. Melissa tentatively tried the handle. To her delight, the door opened inwards, into another small storeroom. It was almost empty but there were two strong bolts on the door. Melissa slipped inside and drew the bolts. At the very worst, her abductors would have to create a noise to recapture her, and she wouldn't go quietly! At the best, they would presume that she had escaped!

She waited, hardly daring to breathe.

The first sign of action was a rattling of the outer door, followed by the sound of the door being kicked in and shouting. Melissa held her breath. She couldn't hear the words clearly but she knew her two abductors were arguing between themselves, each blaming the other. The handle of her hiding place rattled and the door shuddered as a body heaved against it. Another voice joined in the shouting and, eventually, the voices faded away.

Then a male voice called through the door.

'You can come out now. They've gone!'

Melissa lifted her head. It sounded like the attendant from the shop, but, what if her abductors were still there? The young man might be in league with them! No, that would be too great a coincidence.

'I know you're in there! There's no other way out!'

She heard a chuckle.

'Those two dumbos believed you had got out through the window! They have gone! Really!'

'Are you sure?'

'Yes, with a trail of smoke behind them!'

She had to believe him. If he were lying, she'd soon know, and if they really had gone, they might come back, so she needed to be away from here! She stood up and slowly slid back the bolts. The young man from the cash desk was there, on his own.

'Come on! I've had to lock up and I need to get back in there. You'd better come with me.'

'I need to get away in case they come back. Can you get a taxi for me?'

'I can do one better than that! I'm off duty in ten minutes. I'll take you home or wherever you want to go. You can trust me. My ugly mug is on all the videotapes. My name's Joe, by the way.'

Melissa smiled. He wasn't ugly. He was quite good-looking, in fact. She had no alternative but to trust him. She was on edge, however, as they returned to the front of the garage. While Joe was unlocking the door, she anxiously faced the road, dreading to see the same car return.

'Boyfriend trouble, was it?' Joe asked. 'They don't look quite your sort.'

'You can say that again!'

She made a wry grimace. He did deserve some sort of explanation.

'I met them at a nightclub last week. They didn't like it when I told them where to get off, but they found out where I work and bundled me into their car. It was a bit scary, I can tell you! I just want to get out of here.'

'You'd better give the police a call. They might come after you again.'

'Maybe I will,' she agreed, though she knew she wouldn't, not yet.

Oh, she wished Trent were at home. He'd know what to do!

A car drew up outside. Melissa glanced at it in alarm, but it was a different car.

'That's my relief,' Joe said. 'I won't be long. Loiter behind the sweets bar over there, until we've done the hand-over.'

It was a nervy five minutes but at last Melissa was heading back to the city. She decided she had to tell Joe her address because she didn't want to break the journey anywhere. The sooner she was safe inside the flat, the better.

'Whew!' Joe whistled, as he drew up outside Crompton Court. 'I knew you were class but I didn't expect this! I was going to ask if I could see you again but I think you're out of my league!'

Melissa laid her fingers on his arm.

'No, I'm not, but I do have a boyfriend whom I care about very much. I'm very grateful to you. You've been a real pal, Joe. Thank you!'

Joe smiled rucfully.

'You know where to find me if you ever change your mind. See you sometime!

Melissa got out and stood until the car had disappeared. She then hurried inside. It wouldn't be too difficult for Lenny and his henchmen to discover where she was living. Maybe they already knew. Just in case, she avoided the lift and ran lightly up the stairs but all was quiet. It was a relief to be back in the flat. She double-locked the door, determined not to open it for anything! She felt very uneasy. What sort of life had she lived, that these events were happening? Why didn't she remember any of it?

She popped a quick meal into the microwave oven and sat watching the news on the television as she ate it. The realisation that her abduction could have turned into a newsworthy event was a sobering thought. She switched off the television and ran a shower. Washing the day's grit out of her hair and off her body went some way to restoring her inner balance.

She lifted her face up to the spray of warm, clean water, letting it run down her face and through her hair. The scent of the shower gel soothed her. It wasn't her favourite scent but Melissa liked it. She froze. She turned off the shower and slowly picked up the stylish plastic bottle. It wasn't hers! It was Melissa's!

She wasn't Melissa! So, who was she?

She didn't remember wrapping the towel around her hair or putting on her bathrobe — Melissa's bathrobe, she corrected herself. She was sitting on the low stool in front of the dressing-table, staring at her reflection. She unwound the towel and shook out her hair. Slowly, she picked up the hairbrush and began to brush through her hair. Who was she?

She looked at the reflection of the bedroom. No wonder none of it had seemed familiar! This wasn't her home! These clothes weren't hers! Her fingers flew to cover her mouth. Trent wasn't her boyfriend!

A bleep sounded from her shoulder bag. A message had arrived on her mobile phone. It must be Trent, or did Lenny know her number? She pulled out her phone and clicked on to the message.

It read, **Maddie.**

Her eyebrows puckered. Maddie? Maddie? Madeleine! It was her! Her name was Madeleine! Madeleine Fielding — Melissa was her twin sister, her identical twin sister!

She laughed in relief. She wasn't going out of her mind! And she wasn't suffering from schizophrenia! She was an identical twin, but not the one she was supposed to be. Her relief changed to bewilderment. How had she come to be here in Melissa's place? And where was Melissa?

She looked at the phone in her hand and clicked on to read the message.

In a spot of bother! Need you here. Hotel Splendide, Marseille. Don't tell Trent. X Mel.

8

Madeleine stared at the text message. Melissa obviously knew that she was here in her place, and that she was masquerading as her twin. How had it happened?

She frowned as she tried to remember. The accident! That was the start of it. She had banged her head and couldn't remember who or where she was. What had she been doing just before the accident? The memory of the sound of a racing-car engine and squeal of brakes made her clap her hands over her ears. She heard the thud and the bang as the car hit her and she landed on its bonnet and slid off on to the road. She heard a voice scream her name. It was Melissa's voice! Her twin had been there as well. She remembered sitting up and looking at a pretty girl with blonde hair.

She had said, 'I'm all right,' and then she had blacked out.

Her mind leaped backwards now. Melissa had wanted her to change places with her to visit their parents, but she had refused. It had been too outrageous! An outrageous deception! Madeleine grimaced. It seemed Melissa had gone ahead with it anyway, and not only to deceive their parents! She had left her to face an unknown boyfriend and work situation! How like Melissa to flout all conventions and sisterly bonds.

And now she was in a spot of bother! Whatever she had been up to over here, something big enough to have Lenny hot on her heels and to make her run back to Marseille, she hadn't escaped her own talent for getting into trouble. And what was this about having no family? Trent had no idea that Melissa had a twin sister, that was for sure, or that their parents were very much alive! Thank goodness they were away on holiday and had no idea that she and Melissa had been involved in an accident! They would have been frantic with worry.

They were due home any day now and they would expect her to be in touch with them. She paused to consider. Whatever Melissa had done, there was no point in worrying Mum and Dad with it. Melissa had said that it was a few months since she had been in touch. She would leave a message on their answer phone to let them know they weren't forgotten and leave it at that for now.

She stabbed out their number and listened to the dialling tone. The phone rang a number of times and then the answer phone kicked in. She left a quick message, just to say that she was coming home to see them soon but was joining Melissa in France for a couple of days, because there was no doubt about it! Melissa had begged for help and there was no way she could refuse.

Did she have enough money for a return ticket to Marseille? She hadn't spent much since her return from Italy.

Italy! Of course! That was where she had been! She'd been in Italy for about a year, working for Fabia Romayne, Fabia Galliano now! Oh, and the memories were flooding back! And, yes, it was Fabia's wedding on the television the other night. She had been right! She had been there! Oh, she suddenly felt so much happier. It was like coming out of a long, dark tunnel, except she wasn't quite out of it yet!

Melissa didn't want Trent to know about it. Did that mean Melissa wanted to pick him up from where she left off? The thought stabbed at her heart. Melissa was treating Trent badly. Did she really love him? Madeleine didn't know. She, Madeleine, loved him, only she couldn't ever tell him, because he obviously loved Melissa. What a mix-up!

And what could she say about her absence? She couldn't just walk out of the flat without leaving an explanation. What if Trent came back before Melissa did? He would wonder what had become of her. He might even involve the police if he suspected Lenny might be involved. And how was Melissa going to explain her protracted absence? That's if Melissa did indeed intend to come back. Knowing her sister as well as she did, nothing was certain!

She needed some answers from Melissa before she went any further. She dialled her sister's mobile phone number and listened to the dialling tone ringing on and on. She frowned. Melissa obviously wasn't going to answer. Her mind still in turmoil, Madeleine telephoned the airport and booked her ticket, using her credit card to pay for it. Melissa's card, really, she reflected, wondering if Melissa had been using hers. She remembered to give Melissa's name, since she would be using Melissa's passport, even though, technically, it was illegal. Did Melissa never stop to consider the outcome of her impulsive actions?

Her flight was early the next

morning. She was glad of that. The sooner she was away the better. Melissa had better have a good explanation for it all! She scrolled through her phone to send a message and typed out her arrival time and clicked to send it. To her annoyance, the message came back. Melissa must have switched off her phone. Really! She was the absolute limit!

She then telephoned the office to leave a message on the answer phone there, saying that her memory was returning and she felt that she would fully recover if she returned to the hotel in Marseille for a few days. She left a similar message on a note pad for Trent, in case he returned home first. She propped it up against the telephone. She hated telling lies but couldn't tell the truth, not until she had seen Melissa.

Sleep was a long time in coming, as she went over and over the various threads of the episode in her mind. Had Melissa witnessed the accident and

134

then exchanged their bags and walked away? What was she thinking of? She might have been killed! And if Melissa was running away from Lenny, did it not occur to her that she was leaving her sister in the same danger? She pulled a wry face. Melissa hadn't changed.

Her last sobering thought was that her twin must have been desperate to get away from her problems to do such a thing.

A cool shower refreshed her in the morning and she felt more able to face whatever occurred in the next twenty-four hours. She phoned for a taxi and waited in the foyer. When it came, Alec carried her bag for her.

'Going somewhere nice, Miss Fielding?' he asked.

'I'm just going away for a few days whilst Mr Gresham is away,' she said lightly. 'I should be back by the weekend.'

The flight left on time. She slept a little and idled through a magazine until they were told to fasten their seat belts. Butterflies were fluttering wildly in her stomach. She knew that there was no way the customs officers would be able to detect any discrepancies between her face and Melissa's passport photograph but she couldn't help being nervous. This was breaking the law big time!

They landed in brilliant sunshine. Madeleine went through customs, her heart in her mouth in case some bright customs officer was able to detect her deception. She knew she would never be able to lie her way out of it. Her face always gave her away, unlike Melissa, who could always get away with the most outrageous things! Nothing had changed!

She carefully looked around at the waiting people, hoping that Melissa had thought to ring the airport to find out the times of possible in-flights but Melissa was not to be seen. Madeleine went to the taxi rank and asked for the Hotel Splendide. Hopefully, Melissa would be there to greet her and they would get everything sorted out.

The hotel basked in the sunshine. Madeleine stepped out of the taxi, paid her fare and then turned to look at the building. It lived up to its name. It was five storeys high, set amongst palm trees and beautiful plants, much of its frontage darkened glass that gleamed from the rays of the sun.

A doorman stepped forward to hold open the door for her. He nodded curtly with only a glimmer of a smile.

'Good afternoon, Mademoiselle Fielding. It's good to see you again. Monsieur Leroy wishes to see you immediately. If you will report to Reception, they will let him know of your return.'

'Er, merci.'

Madeleine knew her face had coloured. What now? Should she reveal her true identity, or should she let them continue to think she was Melissa? She had better find out what the problem was before she blew Melissa's cover story. She did have some responsibility for her sister. She grimaced to herself. Hadn't she always? Her constant rôle when they were children had been to sort out Melissa's scrapes, always hoping Melissa would grow up and begin to take some responsibility for herself. Maybe she had done it too often. Well, this was to be the last time, she told herself firmly.

The girl on the reception desk had already picked up the in-house phone before Madeleine reached the desk. Madeleine heard her announcing her arrival, her eyes fixed on Madeleine's face.

'Monsieur Leroy will see you right away, Mademoiselle Fielding,' the girl told her, her lips tight.

Her name label announced that her name was Celine.

'Merci, Celine.'

Madeleine hesitated. Celine obviously expected her to know the way.

'Where is Monsieur Leroy?'

'In his office, of course.'

Celine's eyes glanced to her right as she spoke. Madeleine murmured her thanks again and turned to her left, taking the only corridor in that direction. The first door bore the name label, **Andre Leroy. Directeur.** She knocked lightly and waited.

'Entrez!'

Madeleine opened the door and stepped into the room. Monsieur Leroy regarded her coolly.

'Ah, Mademoiselle Fielding. How good of you to return. Have you brought the money to pay off your room bill?'

Madeleine's heart sank. Just wait until she got her hands on her sister! She swallowed hard.

'Will you remind me of the amount, monsieur?' she asked, playing for time whilst her brain worked on overtime.

'Eight thousand and four hundred francs, mademoiselle.'

Madeleine gulped. She didn't have that amount! Her dismay must have shown on her face.

'I must remind you that your passport will not be returned to you, until you have paid your bill, mademoiselle.'

So, that was Melissa's problem! She couldn't return home, or go anywhere until she had her passport returned, that is, her passport, Madeleine's!

'I must ask you for more time, Monsieur Leroy,' she pleaded. 'I can let you have . . . '

She did a rapid calculation in her head.

'Two thousand five hundred francs. That's just over a quarter,' she added eagerly.

Monsieur Leroy nodded curtly.

'Very well. At least you are showing good intention.'

He held out his hand and Madeleine carefully counted out the notes.

'I will get the rest of the money somehow,' she assured him hesitantly.

She wasn't sure how, but she would have to manage it somehow. Maybe if Trent knew, but, no, not until she had spoken to Melissa and discovered the true facts. Monsieur Leroy sighed heavily.

'I will give you until the end of the week, mademoiselle. If the money hasn't been paid by then, I will inform the police authorities of your debt and put the matter into their hands.'

'Merci, monsieur,' she whispered and stood up to leave.

'I must also remind you not to leave Marseille until your bill has been paid in full, Mademoiselle Fielding. If you do so, it will compound the offence into a deliberate intention to defraud. Do you understand?'

Madeleine nodded her head ruefully. She understood only too well. Her passport was confiscated, Melissa was missing and there was debt of the equivalent of five hundred and forty pounds to be paid before the weekend.

She hurried away from the hotel, wanting to put as much distance as possible between the hotel and herself. She couldn't remember ever feeling so embarrassed in her entire life.

The hotel was situated in a prime position opposite the beach. She made her way there and sat down on the edge of a stone wall to sort herself out. What was she to do? She now had about five hundred francs on her and about one hundred pounds in her bank account — Melissa's bank account, that was. She needed to find somewhere very cheap to stay, and she needed to find Melissa as soon as possible, before she had used the little amount of money that she had.

After that, unless they phoned Trent to ask him to put some money into Melissa's account, they needed to get a job to earn the rest of it.

Where should she start?

9

Trent sank back into his seat on the plane back to Manchester with feelings of satisfaction, tempered with concern. He now knew it wasn't Melissa he had fallen in love with again, but her twin sister, Madeleine.

He wondered that he hadn't realised sooner. Madeleine was so different from Melissa, not in looks — they were indeed identical! But in character and temperament they were poles apart. Melissa was the centre and the surrounding of her existence, whereas Madeleine . . . his lips curved upwards into a smile of remembering. She was calmer, more thoughtful, caring and loving. Would she grow to love him when she eventually knew who she was, or had her reticent manner been because she didn't find him attractive?

His thoughts sobered. Was her lack of

memory as total as she had made out? She had Melissa's passport, credit cards, mobile phone and luggage. How could they be in her possession if she hadn't intended to deceive him? And where was Melissa during all this time? She had now been away for almost six weeks, only two of which had been on official business.

True, she had requested a third week, claiming to be following up a contact she had made but her photographs showed what sort of contact that had been! But she was now three weeks overdue. Was she ill? Had something happened to her, or had she, true to nature, flagrantly stayed away, knowing that Madeleine was taking her place? Did she not know about the accident? If she didn't, then the change-over had happened before the accident took place, which implicated Madeleine, but if she did, she had deliberately abandoned her sister, not caring how badly hurt she might be! How could she do that?

He shook his head sadly. His decision to end their relationship on her return had been soundly based. He took out his wallet and extracted the photograph he had shown to Signora Galliano. She had known. Something about the eyes, she had said, and she was right. Even in Melissa's laughing face, there was a calculating look, an expression that said, 'Look at me! This is my best pose!'

Mind you, it was easy now in hindsight! He hadn't had a clue about it before Signora Galliano had said it. She had known about Madeleine having an identical twin, and that their parents weren't dead, as Melissa had told him! Why had she said that? To make her seem vulnerable and in need of someone to care for her? That had certainly been his reaction to her lack of family. As far as he knew, she hadn't contacted them in the few months he had known her.

He put the photograph away with a sigh. There was still a lot to sort out but at least he now knew which way to proceed. He collected his car from the airport long-stay carpark and drove into the city centre. Melissa . . . no, Madeleine, he had to get used to thinking . . . would be at the office and he would suggest that she finished early and that they went out for a meal, and he would gently begin to tell her what he had learned about her.

* * *

'What do you mean, she's not here?'

His voice was sharper than he had intended but Rebecca's words had taken him by surprise.

'She left a message on the answer phone on Tuesday morning. She has begun to get her memory back and has gone back to France to see if being in the same hotel will jog back the rest.'

Trent frowned. Madeleine hadn't been in France. If her memory was returning, France would do nothing to help! Unless . . . did she know that Melissa was still there? Was she going there to report the success of their scheme?

He felt betrayed. And yet, he thought of the past two and a half weeks and the reawakening of the love he had felt towards the woman he had thought was Melissa. Had he been mistaken about Madeleine? His features softened. No, he was sure he hadn't.

'That's fine, Rebecca. I expect she couldn't get hold of me to let me know personally. My mobile phone has been playing up.'

Now, why should he feel he had to lie for her? He knew why. He hoped they still had a future together and he wanted to preserve Madeleine's reputation in the office.

Trent spent an hour or so catching up on the trading situation of the past three days. He was pleased with Madeleine's compilation of the new brochure. It was professionally done and he was sure she had a future in that line of business. Fabia Galliano had also sung her praises.

By mid-afternoon, he was glad to call it a day and return home early to the flat. He needed to decide what to do. He was relieved to see the note propped up against the telephone. At least Madeleine hadn't just gone without leaving word. He read it through, disappointed that it was more or less a repeat of what Rebecca had told him. He had hoped for more.

He tapped the folded note against the palm of his hand. He was sure Madeleine's memory loss had been genuine. Did she now know who she was? If she did, she must have gone to France to see, or find, Melissa. Was Melissa in trouble? The incidents with Lenny had been the outcome of Melissa's dealings here in Manchester. Was she also in trouble in France? What else could have drawn Madeleine there so suddenly?

He looked at his watch. There was no point dashing off there tonight, but, first thing in the morning, he was going to follow Madeleine to France. He

148

pressed the answer phone button. The musical voice announced that he had one message. Trent listened eagerly, hoping it would be Madeleine, but it wasn't.

'Mr Gresham? Inspector Davenport, City Centre Police Station. Will you get in touch as soon as possible? We have information regarding Miss Fielding's accident three weeks ago.'

Trent immediately dialled the given number and asked for the inspector.

'Mr Gresham? Thank you for calling.'

'What's this about, Inspector?'

'We have finally had some eyewitness reports on the hit-and-run accident that Miss Fielding was involved in and have traced the registration number. It belongs to a car owned by a Mr Leonard Rawlings. He is well known to us, mainly drugs. Typical gangster.'

'I've met him. He made threats against Made . . . Miss Fielding, but we don't know in what connection. Her memory, you know . . . '

'Quite! Well, he seems to have gone

underground since the night before last, but we're out looking for him. Just make sure Miss Fielding isn't left on her own until we have apprehended him.'

'Miss Fielding has gone back to France, Inspector Davenport, and I'm not sure exactly where or why.'

'We'll alert all ports and airports, but we might be too late. If you have any idea where she might have gone, I'd appreciate your co-operation.'

'Probably Marseille, The Hotel Splendide. Beyond that, I've no idea.'

* * *

Madeleine perched herself on the high bar stool and ordered a glass of lime and soda, slipping her feet out of her sandals and flexing her ankles. She had tramped around the streets for about three hours, boldly approaching bartenders in bars and restaurants to ask if they needed any extra help. She had grown used to appraising looks that brought a blush to her cheeks and had fended off unwanted offers as firmly as she could.

A few establishments had wanted to take on staff on long-term positions, which she had turned down, wanting to get this over with and return to England as soon as she had found Melissa and helped her to sort out her problem, which included getting back her own passport.

This was her last hope. She looked around the bar as she waited for her drink to be brought to her. It was a pavement café, in one of the side streets away from the sea front, but it had one thing in its favour over any other she had seen on her search. There was a notice outside that declared that temporary staff was needed.

It was already quite busy. There were fifteen tables inside and another dozen or so outside under brightly-coloured parasols. She counted twenty bar stools. The various menus showed that they served a moderate variety of bar meals and the usual selection of wines and spirits. Only two servers were on duty, a girl and a young man. Both looked rushed off their feet.

'You look busy!' Madeleine remarked, as the bar-tender placed the cool glass in front of her.

'You can say that again! And it will become even busier in another hour! I am two staff members down tonight. One has gone to her grandmother's funeral and will be back in two days. The other slipped on some food on the floor and has twisted his ankle.'

'I saw the notice outside. I'm looking for temporary work. Is it a live-in position?'

'It could be. It's only a small attic-room.'

He glanced over the bar at her flight bag.

'Is that all you've got?'

'Yes. I'm in-between jobs and thought I'd stop off here for a few days. I'm looking for my sister.'

'Gone missing, has she?'

Madeleine shrugged, not wanting to make a big issue out of it.

'She phoned me the other day, but forgot to give me her address. I expect she'll be in touch again. What hours would you want me to do?'

'You can have some time off in the mornings once everything is set up and an hour or so late afternoon if we're not busy. Will that do you?'

'I expect so. What wage will I get?'

The sum the man mentioned wasn't very much, Madeleine realised with a sinking heart. It would take a few weeks to pay off Melissa's debt, unless she found Melissa and combined their wages, if Melissa was also working.

'Have you any experience?'

'Not exactly,' Madeleine admitted, 'but I've eaten plenty of meals in restaurants!'

'An excellent recommendation,' the bar-tender said dryly. 'When can you start?'

'Right now!' Madeleine said without any hesitation.

'You're on! My name's Henri.'

'Madeleine Fielding, but call me Maddie.'

'Right, Maddie, tuck your bag under here and go into the kitchen for an apron. Hey, Sabine! Jacques! This is Maddie! She's joining the fray. Show her what she needs to know.'

Madeleine lost track of time. Never again would she underestimate the job of a waitress. From showing customers to their table, handing them the menu, welcoming new customers, returning to the previous ones for their order, to answering queries about the menu, serving the meals, welcoming yet more customers, offering the dessert menu and, finally, handing them the bill and wishing them good-night, there seemed to be no end in sight!

As the last customers left the restaurant at one thirty in the morning, she sank on to a chair.

'Just let me die quietly,' she groaned.

She was too tired to join in the late meal. Thankful that she had eaten snacks as she worked, she crawled up the narrow stairs to the attic bedroom, showered without opening her eyes and dropped on to the bed. At least she had a bed, meals on the job and a chance to find her sister.

She awakened early, breakfasted on croissants and coffee and set off to walk the side streets in the hope of finding someone who knew Melissa. She didn't need to take a photograph. Disappointed by her lack of success, she returned to Henri's in time for her lunchtime shift. The town was so large. Melissa might not even still be here, but she had to persevere.

Her two hours off during the afternoon brought no greater success. Part way through the evening, however, the scene changed. A young man came into the café bar and perched on one of the high stools.

Madeleine turned to serve him. She knew straightaway that her luck was in! The young man was staring at her.

'Melissa? What are you doing here?

Have you left Le Chat Noir?'

'You know my sister?'

Her heart was thumping wildly.

'Your sister?'

'Yes, my twin sister, Melissa. I'm Madeleine, her identical twin. I need to find her. Do you know where she is?'

10

Trent parked his hire car in front of the Hotel Splendide and strode inside. He stood for a moment and stared up at the hotel frontage. Hopefully, since Rebecca said Madeleine had given her the name and phone number of the place, she would have booked in here. He frowned slightly. Did she know she was Madeleine, or would she have booked in as Melissa?

'Ah, bonjour Monsieur Gresham!' the receptionist greeted him warmly. 'You 'ave come to sort out the leetle contretemps, yes?'

Trent smiled disarmingly.

'Hopefully,' he agreed. 'Is it convenient for me to see Monsieur Leroy in say, half an hour?'

He needed a cool shower before he did anything else!

'Certainly, monsieur. I will let him

know you are here.'

She handed him a magnetic key card for his room.

After a cool shower and a change of clothing, Trent felt much refreshed and he made his way to the ground floor and the manager's office. Monsieur Leroy was waiting for him. They shook hands cordially and Trent seated himself in the offered chair. He felt very much disadvantaged. He didn't want to give away any more of his lack of knowledge of the situation than he needed to. He smiled at the man opposite him.

'It's very good of you to see me so readily, Monsieur Leroy. Has Miss Fielding re-booked herself into the hotel in the past two days?'

'She was not so foolhardy as to try, Mr Gresham. I presume she has informed you of her monetary problem?'

Trent frowned slightly, wondering which of the two girls he was referring to. If she had monetary problems it must be Melissa.

'Er, not exactly,' he began, 'though I gathered that there had been a problem. Could you tell me exactly what that problem is?'

'A matter of almost six thousand francs,' Monsieur Leroy stated.

Trent controlled his features, determined not to give away any of his anxiety about Madeleine or Melissa. He automatically converted the amount into sterling. It could have been worse, he supposed.

'How did the amount accrue? Miss Fielding's hotel bill was paid for her for the duration of the conference.'

'She took advantage of a special offer we were running at the time and stayed on for an extra week at half price for the room and paying for meals consumed on the premises. Then, after a brief departure, she returned and booked in for another week. After a . . . shall we say . . . a minor incident in the public bar, when some items of hotel crockery were broken, I demanded instant payment and, when she admitted she hadn't got enough money to pay, I demanded her passport as surety until payment was made. She came here two days ago and paid two thousand five hundred francs. The rest, she promised to bring to me before the end of the week. If the outstanding amount is not paid, I intend to put it into the hands of the police. We do not expect such occurrences from our regular clients, Monsieur Gresham.'

'Of course not. There was some slip-up in communications, monsieur.'

The last contact must have been Madeleine. Melissa would have avoided the place! That meant Madeleine was indeed here in Marseille.

'I will, of course, pay the full amount right now, monsieur.'

He handed over his credit card.

'Please take the full amount from my card, and any extra you require for the inconvenience caused.'

'That will not be necessary, Monsieur

Gresham. Your business has always been valued, and, I hope, you will continue to be a visitor.'

He took the proffered card and pressed a buzzer on his desk. His secretary appeared immediately and took away his card to do the transaction in her office.

'Did Miss Fielding say what she would be doing to . . . er . . . pay off the debt? I presume she would need to obtain some sort of employment, since she couldn't come home to England without her passport.'

Trent needed as much help as he could get, in order to find both of them, he realised, since Madeleine must have come here to help Melissa. Had they become reunited yet, he wondered.

Monsieur Leroy was shaking his head.

'No, monsieur, though I understood her to mean she intended to get a job somewhere. But where, I do not know. What shall I do with Miss Fielding's passport?'

He reached down to unlock a drawer in his desk.

'May I see it?' Trent asked.

'Certainly.'

He handed it across his desk. As Trent had presumed, it was Madeleine's passport. Melissa had got hold of it somehow, but was it with or without Madeleine's knowledge and consent? Monsieur Leroy obviously hadn't been aware of the different Christian name. Trent's gaze softened as he looked at the beloved face. What would Madeleine do next? She had two days in which to earn some money, but never the amount required! She might return with whatever she had managed to earn, and hope for an extension of times. He met Monsieur Leroy's gaze.

'I have no right to keep Miss Fielding's passport, even though I have paid her debt. What I must ask is that you let me know if she returns with the money, or part of it, and try to delay her until I can meet with her. She is in my employ and I feel some responsibility towards her.'

He took out his wallet and extracted a small card.

'Here is my mobile phone number.'

Monsieur Leroy nodded.

'I will do as you ask, monsieur, though I cannot guarantee to keep her here against her will, not now that the debt has been paid.'

Trent nodded in agreement. It would not be easy to track either of the twins down, especially if they remained apart, but he would do his best.

*　*　*

Madeleine awakened early the next morning. She had thought she wouldn't sleep with the excitement of knowing where Melissa was working but she had, eventually! She rushed through the early-morning preparations for morning coffee, helping in the preparation of numerous croissants and other pastries and had then set off to find Le Chat

Noir, and, hopefully, Melissa. She glanced down at the piece of paper in her hand where she had written the address and directions.

She felt a mixture of exhilaration and apprehension as she walked quickly along the already sun-baked streets. What was she going to discover about her sister? Why was she so much in debt? And where exactly did Lenny Rawlings fit in? The thought of her own narrow escape from his men still made her feel distinctly uneasy. What if they had somehow followed her to the flat and from there to the airport?

'Stop being so jittery!' she scolded herself.

All the same, she would be glad when she had a few answers. She just hoped that Melissa was there! Le Chat Noir was a similar establishment to the one she was working at. Some customers were seated at some of the outside tables and a harassed, dark-haired waitress was hurrying amongst them. Madeleine threaded her way through the tables and into the cool interior. She could hear sounds of voices coming from the kitchen beyond the counter.

She called out, 'Hello! Is anyone there?'

Eventually, a middle-aged man, a white apron tied around his middle, appeared in the open doorway. Madeleine saw his face change from enquiry to annoyance as he recognised her face.

'What are you doing, mademoiselle, bringing me to the front? You know you should come in at the back! I haven't got time to be running after you like this. There is much work to be done. Get into the kitchen and start shaping the croissants. We have clients already waiting to be served. They will not wait all day.'

Madeleine couldn't get a word in until he paused for an answer.

'Bonjour, monsieur. I am not Melissa. I am her twin sister, Madeleine.'

She laughed at his surprised expression.

'We are very alike, I know. I would like to see my sister, but I presume she isn't in.'

'She went out . . . asked for time off to go to see someone.'

He stared at her suspiciously.

'Are you sure you aren't her?'

'Absolutely sure, monsieur! Do you know where she went?'

He lifted his hands in a negative gesture.

'A young man came in last night and spoke to her. She was very excited. Wanted to leave immediately but I needed her here. She went out about half an hour ago and promised to be back very quickly. You tell her that I want reliable staff. I will not put up with this.'

Madeleine tried to look apologetic.

'I'm sorry! She has probably gone to see me. Merci! I must return to where I am staying! Au revoir, monsieur!'

With a slight wave of her hand, she left immediately and began to hurry back. They must have passed each other en route. Cross though she felt with Melissa for getting them both into this situation, she was excited at the thought of meeting her again at last. As she turned a corner, she could see Melissa across the street, hurrying in her direction.

'Melissa!' she called.

Melissa turned her head and stared across at her, a wide smile spreading across her face.

'Maddie!'

Madeleine had already made sure the road was clear and was hurrying across the road. They met just off the other pavement, hugging each other, oblivious to other pedestrians and the few passing cars. It was Madeleine who brought the hug to an end. She stood back.

'Mel, you've got to tell me what this is all about. Do you realise what you've done to me? I've been thinking I was going out of my mind! Are you in some sort of trouble?'

Melissa looked up and down the

street as if afraid of being overheard.

'Yes. Oh, Maddie, I've been so stupid. And then I got frightened, and while I was here in Marseille, I met the most marvellous man and didn't want to leave him, only Trent was expecting me back. There's also someone else in England I'm keeping away from because I think he's after me. Then I ran up a hotel bill I couldn't pay and your passport got confiscated and I knew I couldn't leave without it.'

Her words tumbled out on top of each other, her expression reminding Madeleine of many a childhood scrape from which she had rescued her.

'But, Melissa, you left me after a road traffic accident, and I was in hospital for a week with a lost memory!'

Madeleine shook her head in disbelief. Had Melissa really no concept of the severity of what she had done? Obviously not!

'I didn't know who I was!' she continued. 'And everyone thought I was you. I thought I was going out of my mind. What on earth made you do it?'

Melissa's hand flew to cover her mouth.

'But, you seemed all right, Maddie. I asked you if you were all right and you said yes.'

'So you switched our bags and ran.'

'I was desperate, Maddie. I needed time to find out if I preferred Damien or Trent, and I was scared of what Lenny might do to me when he caught up with me. I really needed to get away for a while.'

'Didn't it occur to you that Lenny might think I was you, and try to harm me? What exactly have you been up to, Melissa?'

'Yes, Melissa! I, too, would like to know that!'

The deep, masculine voice cut into their conversation. Both girls froze for a split second. It was Trent! Neither of them had noticed his approach, so engrossed were they in hearing what the other had to say. They turned to face him, their faces mirror images of shocked dismay.

Trent looked from one to the other and his eyes narrowed.

'Well, girls, you certainly had me fooled. So, whose idea was it? Melissa's or Madeleine's?'

Madeleine felt a stab of fear that paralysed her mind and froze her body. Her head began to turn, following the line of Trent's sudden fixed gaze. A red car was hurtling straight towards them and her bewildered mind partly registered that Lenny Rawlings was at the wheel.

11

The next few seconds were like a slow-action replay as Trent lunged forward at both girls, grabbing one in each arm as he dived in a rugby tackle taking both of them crashing to the ground. Madeleine knew that the car had miraculously missed them. A loud bang, that seemed to blow up the whole world, exploded around them, followed by a shower of tiny sharp crystals.

Madeleine felt as though every bone in her body had been jolted out of place. She had banged her head against the pavement but didn't lose consciousness. She could hear screaming and the acrid smell of fire and smoke. Trent's body was on top of her. She sensed, rather than knew, that Melissa was curled up beside her, burrowing under her for protection.

She lost all sense of time. At some

point, hands pulled the weight of Trent's body off them and other hands dragged them away from the immediate vicinity of the blazing car. She became aware of a babble of voices. Trent was crouched at their side. Thank goodness he was alive! She had feared the blast had killed him. She felt the comfort of his fingers stroking her face.

'It's all right! You're both all right!' his voice soothed.

The sirens of police and ambulance vehicles forced a path through the gathering crowds and Madeleine was thankful to let everything just happen around them.

They, and others at the scene, were taken to the nearest hospital and underwent examination and treatment for numerous cuts by flying glass, inhalation of smoke and shock. Both girls were beginning to bruise but neither had suffered concussion and they were eventually discharged from the hospital with warnings to return if they began to suffer severe headaches or loss of consciousness.

It was much later, when the questioning by the police was over, and they were seated in Trent's suite of rooms at the hotel that the full story became clear. Leonard Rawlings had driven a car straight at them and they had only been saved by Trent's quick action of flinging them out of its path. Lenny was dead, probably from the impact of the car into the building, though the ferocity of the fire made it impossible for the rescuers to be absolutely certain of that.

After they had eaten a light meal, reluctantly at first, Melissa finally revealed her side of the story.

'Yes, I took drugs! So what? Everyone does at some time or other!' she said defiantly. 'I bet you have!'

Madeleine shook her head.

'No, I haven't. It's playing with fire. Some people die from using drugs. Even if they don't kill you, they have such detrimental effects.'

'Well, I only used soft ones, and I

always intended to stop before I became addicted to them, and I did! Only, by then, I was in debt to Lenny Rawlings. He said he had a way out for me, if I acted as a courier to bring a small packet into the country. He paid me in advance, but when I saw the size of the packet and worked out its street value I had second thoughts about it and wanted out. I was scared. What if I got caught? I tried to return the package but Lenny refused to take it. He said he would make sure that evidence against me would fall into the hands of the Drugs Squad if I didn't work for him! He insisted that the package had been opened and a quantity was missing, to the cost of two thousand pounds. But I hadn't! Honestly!'

Madeleine believed her. She always knew when Melissa was lying and now she definitely wasn't, without a doubt.

'So, what happened?'

'Lenny wouldn't accept my denial. I was really frightened and when Trent mentioned the international Wine Merchants' Conference I knew it would give me a breathing space whilst I decided what to do, but it wasn't long enough! When we met so coincidentally at the airport, it seemed too fortunate to let it pass.'

Melissa's brilliant blue eyes glistened with unshed tears as she turned to Trent, smiling tremulously at him.

'I was a fool to think I preferred Damien to you, darling. When I returned here he seemed pleased at first, but after a week or so he attached himself to some bimbo or other, only, by then, I couldn't afford to pay my hotel bill, and Monsieur Leroy confiscated my passport.'

She smiled apologetically at Madeleine.

'Your passport, Madeleine,' she corrected herself. 'I couldn't return to England without it, and I knew it would take me ages to earn that much money on my own.'

She reached out to touch Madeleine's hand.

'I knew you would be filling my place admirably, but not with Trent, of course! I knew I could trust you, Maddie! You always were the more admirable one of us.'

Her silvery laugh tinkled around, her eyes now dancing with merriment, and Madeleine felt her face freeze as Melissa continued.

'I knew you would come out to help me. I needed you to help me pay my hotel bill and to bring my real passport. You'd said you didn't have a job, so no-one would miss you if you came out there for a while, would they? And I knew that once I was back home, Trent would pay you back for me.'

She turned to Trent and smiled beguilingly at him.

'Now you're here, you will pay Monsieur Leroy for me, won't you, darling?'

'I have already done so,' he said quietly.

Madeleine could bear no more.

'Excuse me,' she said, standing up.

'You've obviously got a lot to talk about. I'd better be going. I just need to use the bathroom, if that's all right.'

It was the only excuse she could think of. Her body ached, but the ache in her heart was worse.

She washed her face, patting some powder around her puffed eyes. She critically surveyed her reflection, pulling a rueful expression. It was only to be expected, she supposed. Melissa was more vibrant and exciting than she was, and now she wanted to reclaim her handsome boyfriend. Trent must be equally delighted to have her back. He had come all this way and had already paid Melissa's debt. He must love her very much.

She had noticed how puzzled he had looked at times. No wonder! She must have been a severe disappointment to him after Melissa's natural vivacity. Madeleine stared bleakly at herself in the mirror. She must get away as soon as she was able. Maybe she should return to Henri's café? It was early evening and he must be wondering what had become of her. She didn't really feel up to working but it would take her mind off everything. Yes, that's what she'd do.

It was only as she came out of the bathroom and into the small hallway. that she realised that Melissa had followed her from the sitting-room.

'I had to follow you, Maddie. You seemed upset,' Melissa said.

She took in Madeleine's red eyes and grinned in understanding.

'Don't say you've fallen for Trent whilst I was away. You goose! He's such a dear and has probably made you feel he really cares for you, but it was only because he thought you were me! You'll get over it, love. There's a man out there for you somewhere. You'll find him, given time.'

Madeleine nodded hopelessly. Maybe, but, right now, the only man she wanted was Trent Gresham.

'Come on! Let's go back to him. He'll be wondering what's keeping us.

Thank goodness I don't need to work in that dreadful street café any more. And you, too, Maddie. I'm sure Trent will book you in here as well. He's so generous. Then we can exchange our passports and everything and decide whether or not to stay on for a few days. It's such a gorgeous place.'

Melissa tucked her hand into Madeleine's arm. Madeleine hesitated.

'I think I'd rather go back to the café bar, if you don't mind. They're short-staffed and I'd rather feel useful than act as a gooseberry to you and Trent.'

Melissa pouted but immediately brightened as she released her hold on Madeleine.

'Well, all right, if you're sure.'

She grinned impishly.

'It will give Trent and me the chance to catch up on lost time.'

Trent was standing by the window overlooking the seafront. His face looked uncharacteristically stern as he turned to face them. Madeleine avoided his eyes. She felt embarrassed by her own obvious distress. She held out her hand towards him, hoping her farewell would be brief and painless. She would return to their family home as soon as her commitment to Henri was completed and she would eventually pick up the pieces of her life. Did broken hearts mend quickly, she wondered.

She could hardly bear to look at Trent, though she wanted to carry his image in her heart for a while longer. The softened expression in his eyes almost broke her resolve to leave immediately. She felt there was something left unsaid between them but he merely squeezed her hand tightly.

'I've just booked you a room here,' Trent said as she withdrew her hand from his.

'But . . . ' she began but was interrupted before she could say anything.

'No arguments! If you'll tell me the name of the café you were working in, I'll phone the owner and explain what has happened. You're in no condition to work until midnight or beyond, so don't even think of arguing.'

'But, I've no clothes here, nor any toiletries!'

'Everything you need will be in your room, and I'll arrange for a couple of new outfits to be purchased for you to wear tomorrow. Haven't you noticed what a state your dress is in?'

No, she hadn't, but he obviously had!

'What did I tell you?' Melissa said and grinned triumphantly at her sister. 'Isn't he a dear?'

Trent picked up the hotel phone and spoke rapidly into it.

'A maid will be along directly,' he said, as he replaced the receiver. 'I will see you tomorrow.'

There was a quiet tap at the door even as he finished speaking and a rather bemused Madeleine trailed miserably along the plush corridor after the young woman. The last words she had heard as the door closed after her were from Melissa.

'I've missed you so much, Trent. I was beginning to think we'd never be alone.'

Madeleine gasped as she entered her room. It was another suite like Trent's. It was beautiful. The thick cream carpet was soft under her feet as she kicked off her sandals and followed the maid into a sumptuous bedroom with its en-suite bathroom.

'I will run the bath for you, mademoiselle,' the maid offered.

Madeleine thanked her as she picked up the satin nightdress that lay on the bed. The maid waited whilst she bathed, holding out a luxurious bath-sheet as she rose from the water.

'And now, a soothing massage, mademoiselle, and then you will sleep, yes?'

'Yes,' Madeleine agreed.

She suddenly realised just how tired she was.

'I am to keep looking in on you through the night, mademoiselle,' the maid explained, 'but I will do my best not to disturb you. Monsieur Gresham is anxious in case you suffer from concussion.'

Madeleine was too tired to protest. She didn't expect to sleep, but she did. She awoke early, to the feeling of unaccustomed luxury as she stretched out in the bed.

'Ooh!'

Her muscles protested as she moved. That hurt! She moved again. That was better! She eased herself upward and swung her legs over the side of the bed. A refreshing shower, a quick breakfast and she would be off. Hanging in the wardrobe was a selection of dresses, trousers, tops and shorts with matching shoes and an assortment of lacy underwear was in the drawers. She shook her head in silent wonder. She didn't need all this, but it was nice, she decided.

The maid smiled at her surprise.

'Monsieur Gresham sent them up to the room. There is a note.'

She handed it to Madeleine.

Madeleine's fingers trembled as she opened it.

I hope you had a good night. We need to talk. I will come in half an hour's time. Trent.

She couldn't face him, not yet. She needed more time. As soon as she was dressed she had to go. She chose one of the dresses to wear and slipped her feet into a pair of shoes. They fitted exactly, as did the dress. How wonderful to have a man who knew exactly your size and could choose dresses that you liked. Melissa was very fortunate. Madeleine hoped she wouldn't spoil things for herself by being too selfish and grasping.

She contemplated saying goodbye to Melissa before she left but decided against it. Melissa wasn't an early riser and she was probably still in bed. She would leave a message at Reception and arrange to meet her later in the day to exchange the passports.

The corridors were almost deserted as she made her way to the nearest lift.

She pressed the button to bring it rising up from the lower floors. The door slid back and she stepped forward.

'Oh!' she exclaimed.

Trent was about to step forward out of the lift. They were both surprised.

No wonder, Madeleine thought. Melissa wouldn't be up and about for ages yet. Trent stepped forward.

'Where are you going?' he asked softly, as the lift door slid back into place.

He didn't wait for an answer. Instead, he wrapped his arms around her and lightly kissed her mouth. It was bitter-sweet. For a delicious moment she melted into him. Surely it wouldn't be too wrong to savour the last kiss she would have from him? As his kiss lightened, she pulled away.

'You've got the wrong one, Trent. I'm Madeleine, not Melissa,' she said shakily.

Trent pulled her closer again.

'I know who you are,' he said softly, 'and you're the right one for me, if you'll have me!'

The joy Madeleine felt was instantly vanquished.

'But . . . '

'Melissa has gone. We had a talk last night.'

He thought fleetingly of the loud scene of threats and recriminations. He shook his head sadly.

'It was already over between us. I was just giving her her ticket home. I was sorry it had to be like this. I had intended to speak to her privately on our return to England but I couldn't just stand by and let her speak to you as she had just done. And I couldn't wait that long to hold you in my arms.'

He looked lovingly down at her.

'What do you think? Do you think you could grow to love me as much as I love you?'

Madeleine smiled.

'Oh, Trent, I already love you, but what about Melissa?'

She wouldn't be pleased! Melissa liked to be the one to end her relationships. She wouldn't take kindly to being rejected, especially not in favour of her sister.

'I don't think you should worry too much about Melissa Identical twins you may be, but in character, you are poles apart. She'll smart for a little while, but not because she loves me. She doesn't! I've known that since before she went away, and I had stopped loving her long before then. I just hadn't got around to telling her it was over. I suppose I was hoping she would do the finishing. Her pride is hurt, that's all. She'll get over it, and we are all meeting Monsieur Leroy later this morning to sort out the passports. So, what do you say?'

Madeleine smiled and lifted up her face.

'Kiss me again!'

And he did. Madeleine felt her spirits roar. She was safe in the arms of the man she loved and he loved her. The whole outrageous deception was over!

THREE TALL TAMARISKS

Christine Briscomb

Joanna Baxter flies from Sydney to run her parents' small farm in the Adelaide Hills while they recover from a road accident. But after crossing swords with Riley Kemp, life is anything but uneventful. Gradually she discovers that Riley's passionate nature and quirky sense of humour are capturing her emotions, but a magical day spent with him on the coast comes to an abrupt end when the elegant Greta intervenes. Did Riley love Greta after all?

SUMMER IN HANOVER SQUARE

Charlotte Grey

The impoverished Margaret Lambart is suddenly flung into all the glitter of the Season in Regency London. Suspected by her godmother's nephew, the influential Marquis St. George, of being merely a common adventuress, she has, nevertheless, a brilliant success, and attracts the attentions of the young Duke of Oxford. However, when the Marquis discovers that Margaret is far from wanting a husband he finds he has to revise his estimate of her true worth.

CONFLICT OF HEARTS

Gillian Kaye

Somerset, at the end of World War I: Daniel Holley, unhappily married to an ailing wife and father of four grown-up children, is attracted to beautiful schoolteacher Harriet Bray, but he knows his love is hopeless. Daniel's only daughter, Amy, who dreams of becoming a milliner and is caught up in her love for young bank clerk John Tottle, looks on as the drama of Daniel and Harriet's fate and happiness gradually unfolds.

THE SOLDIER'S WOMAN

Freda M. Long

When Lieutenant Alain d'Albert was deserted by his girlfriend, a replacement was at hand in the shape of Christina Calvi, whose yearning for respectability through marriage did not quite coincide with her profession as a soldier's woman. Christina's obsessive love for Alain was not returned. The handsome hussar married an heiress and banished the soldier's woman from his life. But Christina was unswerving in the pursuit of her dream and Alain found his resistance weakening . . .

THE TENDER DECEPTION

Laura Rose

When Sophia Barton was taken from Curton Workhouse to be a scullery-maid at Perriman Court, her future looked bleak. Was it really an act of Providence that persuaded Lady Perriman to adopt her as her ward? Sophia was brought up together with the Perriman children, and before sailing with his regiment for India, George, the heir to the title, declared his love. But tragedy hit the family and Sophia found herself caught up in a web of mystery and intrigue.

CONVALESCENT HEART

Lynne Collins

They called Romily the Snow Queen, but once she had been all fire and passion, kindled into loving by a man's kiss and sure it would last a lifetime. She still believed it would, for her. It had lasted only a few months for the man who had stormed into her heart. After Greg, how could she trust any man again? So was it likely that surgeon Jake Conway could pierce the icy armour that the lovely ward sister had wrapped about her emotions?